"You are obviously determined to screw yourself into a worthy grave," said Sergeant Alfred Brooks.

He sounded disgusted. "Too bad. A left hook is a terrible thing to waste.

His hands were cuffed behind his back to . . . in the small room with the . . . face. Brooks and the little . . . ble.

". . . know you were carrying crack?" asked Brooks.

Sonny stared at the wall. If he said, Yes, he'd be guilty. If he said, No, he'd sound like a fool.

THE BRAVE

Robert Lipsyte

🏛 HarperTrophy®
An Imprint of HarperCollins*Publishers*

The Brave
Copyright © 1991 by Robert M. Lipsyte
All rights reserved. No part of this book may be used or
reproduced in any manner whatsoever without written
permission except in the case of brief quotations embodied in
critical articles and reviews. Printed in the United States of
America. For information address HarperCollins Children's
Books, a division of HarperCollins Publishers, 1350 Avenue of
the Americas, New York, NY 10019.

Library of Congress Cataloging-in-Publication Data
Lipsyte, Robert.
The brave / by Robert Lipsyte.
p. cm.
Sequel to: The contender.
Summary: Having left the indian reservation for the streets of
New York, seventeen-year-old boxer Sonny Bear tries to har-
ness his inner rage by training with Alfred Brooks, who has left
the sport to become a policeman.
ISBN 0-06-447079-2 (pbk.)
1. Indians of North America—Juvenile fiction. [1.Indians of
North America—Fiction. 2. Boxing—Fiction.] I. Title.
PZ7.L67Br 1991   90-25396
[Fic]—dc20   CIP
                                                         AC

Typography by Henrietta Stern
◆
First Harper Trophy edition, 1993
Visit us on the World Wide Web!
www.harperteen.com

FOR KATHY

THE BRAVE

SONNY BEAR SWAGGERED down the aisle, banging his big red gloves together, whipping his black ponytail from side to side against his bare shoulders, feeling the hatred of the crowd slap his body like a fine cold spray. Keep it coming, you hillbilly bozos, thought Sonny. Makes me strong.

He vaulted into the ring, a sudden move that surprised the crowd. No one expected a heavyweight so quick. He raised his fists above his head. The crowd stomped and hooted. Someone shouted, "Gonna need a tommyhawk tonight, Injun," and the bozos laughed. He felt the monster stir in his chest.

The hometown fighter was already in the ring, a big farm boy with curly yellow fur growing over his chest and back. He flexed his lumpy biceps and glared at Sonny. The crowd cheered. The farm boy was Sonny's height, six foot one, but he looked fifty pounds heavier.

Not all of it was fat. He was older, too, at least nineteen. Sonny glared back. The crowd booed.

Jake pulled him back into his corner and pushed him down on his stool. "Here to win. Not make 'em mad." His dry old fingers massaged Sonny's neck.

Sonny checked the crowd. What you'd expect at a Friday-night smoker in a mountain town. A couple hundred white guys on folding chairs sucking on beer cans and talking big. They were in their workday clothes, overalls and greasy jeans and short-sleeved shirts with their nicknames stitched on the chests. The big-mouths who like to give Indians a tough time in hardware stores and gas stations, thought Sonny. If I wasn't wearing gloves, I'd give them the finger. The monster was hot in his throat. Furry farm boy's going to taste some tommy-hawk tonight.

The overhead fluorescent lights blinked off. Spotlights blazed down on the ring. Bells rang. A big man in a white bowling shirt that read HILLCREST MOTOR HOMES on the back raised his beefy arms. "Listen up now, fellas, final match of the evening, heavyweights, two hundred bucks, winner take all. . . . In the black trunks . . ."

2

Boos swamped the ring. A crumpled beer can sailed out of the darkness and landed on the canvas. Crowd's juiced, thought Sonny. The announcer kicked the can out of the ring. The crowd laughed.

". . . weighing one hundred and eighty pounds, youngster's been making a name for himself, five straight wins, from the Moscondaga Reservation, Sonny Bear."

Bells rang to choke back the jeers. The monster filled him.

"In the white trunks . . . weighing two hundred and fifteen pounds . . . the pride of Hillcrest . . . our own . . . Glen Hoffer."

The crowd stood and cheered as Hoffer lumbered into the center of the ring, arms raised. His body hair was golden in the ring lights. He's closer to two fifty than two fifteen, thought Sonny. When he goes down, the whole building's going to shake, rattle and roll.

"Jab," whispered Jake. "Jab and work his belly. No head-hunting."

The announcer beckoned Sonny to the center of the ring. He was going to referee this one, make sure Glen Hoffer didn't get hurt too bad, thought Sonny. Good luck.

3

"Five rounds, anyone gets knocked down twice in one round it's over. Got that?" When they both nodded, he looked directly at Sonny. "No kicking, boy, no gouging, biting, butting, hitting below the belt, none of that reservation stuff."

The ref turned to Hoffer. "After a knockdown, Glen, go right to a neutral corner so's I can start the count."

Back in his corner, just before the bell, Sonny swigged water from Jake's taped bottle and spat it into a bucket. He opened his mouth so Jake could slip in the plastic guard. Jake pushed his dark, wrinkled face close. "Careful, Sonny. Jab and belly." Between his feet was the overnight bag with Sonny's clothes. Good old Great-Uncle Jake, he thought, ready for a fast getaway.

The bell rang.

"No head-hunting," yelled Jake.

Bust that pale face, ordered the monster.

Sonny sprang out and fired the left hook at Hoffer's head before the farm boy got his hands up.

Bingo.

Hoffer's legs kicked out and he crashed to

the deck. He sat on the canvas, an amazed expression on his big, dumb face.

Sonny's laugh woke him up. Hoffer rolled over on his hands and knees. Clumsily, he pushed himself back up to his feet. The referee jumped between them and wiped Hoffer's gloves off on his shirt. Sonny couldn't hear what he said to Hoffer.

The farm boy's cheek was bright red where the hook had landed. There was a drop of blood in one nostril. He raised his gloves to his heaving chest and marched toward Sonny, eyes narrowed, lips tight.

He never expected another hook. To the same spot.

This one turned him around. He staggered into the ropes and fell to his knees. Only his elbows, snagged on the middle rope, kept him up. He hung there like a side of beef. Sonny strolled to a neutral corner. Second knockdown. It's over. Easy payday.

The referee helped Hoffer up. "That was only a slip," he said, "not a knockdown."

The monster snickered, What do you expect, Redskin? A fair fight?

Sonny watched Hoffer lurch toward him,

carried along on a chanting chorus, "Glen . . . Glen . . . Glen," his eyes glazed and his lips slack.

He's out on his feet. One more good shot and he's gone, there's no way they can rob this fight.

"Jab and belly," yelled Jake. "Don't let him come close."

Sonny dug in and let Hoffer come close, into range to catch the full impact of the final punch, a short left hook that would bust that pale white face like a rotten cantaloupe, bust all those pale faces, bury the tommyhawk in every one of them.

C'mon, farmer, I'm gonna plant you now.

He unleashed the hook.

It never landed.

Sonny felt the uppercut graze his thigh before it slammed into his groin and lifted him off his feet. He fell forward, into Hoffer, his legs rubbery. He was swimming into a damp, hairy wall. He couldn't focus. There were three Hoffers. They pushed him away.

Sonny staggered backward, tripped himself, hit the canvas and rolled over on his face. He gasped for air as the pain exploded between his legs and surged up into his belly.

Far away, he heard the referee announce, "Accidental punch, no disqualification, black trunks has thirty seconds to recover."

The bell saved him. Jake dragged him back to his stool, pulled open his trunks and rubbed his chest. He broke a capsule under Sonny's nose. The chemical smell drove into his brain like a hot wire.

His eyes focused. But the pain in his groin and belly had become a deep, thumping ache, and he couldn't feel his feet. He waited for the monster to rise again, to fill him with the anger that fueled him, but there was only a hollow tiredness.

"'S okay," said Jake in his ear. "Pain'll go away. Stick and move till he makes a mistake. He's stupid, afraid of the hook."

"Legs," gasped Sonny. "Can't . . ."

"Got to," growled Jake. "We don't quit in front of these people."

The ref loomed up. "Throwin' in the towel?"

"We came to fight," said Jake.

Across the ring, Hoffer was waving and grinning at his friends. Sonny tried to find the monster, rouse the anger, but it was gone.

Doesn't matter. They were going to rob the fight like they robbed everything else. Why bother? It's not quitting if you don't have a chance in the first place. They make up their own rules as they go along. There's no such thing as an accidental punch. So who cares what these people think?

The bell rang. Jake pushed him out into the ring.

He could have been pole dancing at a pow-wow, his legs felt so long and wooden. His movements were jerky. The best he could do was throw jabs at Hoffer to keep him off balance, keep him from battering him with his bulk, wearing him down. Sonny sidestepped and backpedaled, pushing out the jab. It had lost its snap.

Jake was right. Hoffer was stupid and he was afraid of the hook. He didn't sense how weak Sonny was. One swarming rush and he could finish Sonny, the fight would be over. But the memory of that left hand held him back.

Maybe I should just get this over with, thought Sonny. Let Hoffer hit me with one good punch. Pretend to be knocked out. All go home.

Not in front of these people.

Whose people? I'm an Indian up here, but when the chiefs sit in the Long House and tell their secrets, I'm just a mixed-blood white boy.

The crowd whistled as Sonny and Hoffer shuffled around each other. The ref stepped between them. "Boxing, boys, not dancing." He leaned toward Hoffer. "Go for it, Glen, the Injun's hurt." The farm boy nodded, straightened up.

"Jab," yelled Jake, "jab," as Hoffer marched into him, arms pumping, driving him backward.

Sonny pinned Hoffer's elbows to his sides. Hoffer stamped on his toes, kicked his shins, lowered his head and tried to grind his spiky blond hair into Sonny's face.

"Ref," yelled Jake, "watch that."

"Minute to go," said the ref. "Let's mix it up."

As they stepped apart, Hoffer tried to rub the laces of his gloves in Sonny's eyes. Sonny stuck out a jab to push him away. It popped Hoffer on the nose and snapped his head back.

The punch surprised Sonny as much as it surprised Hoffer. For an instant Hoffer was rocking on his heels. The monster sensed the moment and flooded back into Sonny's body. He hit Hoffer with a right. The farm boy stiffened. Sonny fired the left hook.

Bingo.

Hoffer crashed to the canvas.

The bell rang.

"Round ain't over," yelled Jake. "Twenty more seconds." He was in the ring, shaking his stopwatch under the ref's nose. But the ref ignored Jake as Hoffer's grinning cornermen hoisted him to his feet and rubbed his arms and chest.

Deep inside Sonny the monster chuckled, What do you expect from these people? Read your history books. Cheat and steal and never let you win. He felt a heat that steeled his legs and pumped the muscles of his arms and sent him hurtling across the ring at Hoffer.

He smashed a fist into the middle of the furbag's stupid face.

The big blond flew backward into his corner and crashed into his stool, splintering it. His cornermen reached for Sonny. He hit one of them high on the side of the head. He went down like a sack of grain.

Bells rang, men shouted and ran, the lights went on. It seemed distant to Sonny, a TV movie in another room. He turned in time to see the ref lunging at him. He cocked his left.

"No," yelled Jake, grabbing his arm. He tried to swing at the ref with Jake hanging on, but the skinny old man was heavier and stronger than he looked. White hands were reaching for him, a beer can bounced off his shoulder, men were leaning into the ring trying to hit him.

Jake pushed him through the ropes. Sonny tumbled off the apron to the wooden floor of the lodge hall. Jake pulled him up by the seat of his trunks and shoved him through the crowd. A man in overalls blocked their way. Jake swatted him aside with the overnight bag. They pushed and kicked through the milling bodies to the outside door and burst out of the building into a warm night that fell on Sonny's sweat-slick body like a cold sheet.

They ran through the parking lot and scrambled up into the cab of Jake's tow truck. Men were pounding on the doors as Sonny twisted the ignition key and started kicking the gas pedal. Jake reached into the dashboard, through a tangle of old radio wires, and pulled out his ancient Colt .45. The tow truck roared into life and the mob scattered as Sonny burned rubber out to the road.

Halfway down the mountain, the road forked, left and right.

"Which way?" asked Sonny.

"Don't matter," mumbled Jake. "Both go all the way down. Should have won that fight, Sonny."

"They robbed me."

"Robbed yourself," said Jake. He shoved the revolver back into the dashboard. "Didn't win. Didn't get your money. Worst of all, you gave them a chance to call us a bunch of savages who can't follow the rules."

"They didn't follow the rules," said Sonny.

"They ain't our teachers. We're our teachers." He looked at Sonny. "You let the bad spirit take over."

"Bad spirit." The monster roused. "I'm sick of your dumb Indian talk." He was sorry he said it before it was out.

"You got no control."

"For what?"

"For yourself. For your people." Jake's

voice was sad. "You the last one with the blood of the Running Braves."

"You live on fairy tales."

Jake's mouth snapped shut. Sonny knew he wouldn't talk anymore tonight.

'S okay, old man, thought Sonny. There's nothing more to say. I know what I've got to do now.

HE CLIMBED DOWN from his bunk an hour before dawn, fully dressed except for his boots. Jake's junkyard dogs had stopped barking. Jake would be asleep in front of the TV by now. Sonny hadn't slept at all, but he had never felt so awake.

I'm making my move, he thought. I'm finally getting out of this trap.

He pulled on his green, hand-tooled saddle boots. His mouth was dry, his bowels queasy. That's good. Means I'm ready. He thought of Jake's stories of the great old hunts and battles, the warriors arising in darkness, thanking the Creator for the fears that made their senses super sharp, that gave them control over their bodies. The best of the warriors, the Running Braves, could smell the breath of their prey a mile away, and slow the beating of their hearts so an enemy would mistake them for dead.

C'mon, Sonny, no more fairy tales. This is

just the kind of dumb Redskin lipflap you need to leave behind.

He patted the wallet jammed into a back pocket of his jeans and chained to a belt loop. Its bulge had comforted him all night. It was fat with the Army enlistment papers, the money he had saved from his other smoker fights and the card with his mother's address and phone number in New York. This time he'd make her sign the Army consent form. He'd ambush her if he had to. Just a few more hours. Freedom.

He opened the window, threw his deerskin backpack into the yard and climbed out after it into a clear, cool night. Stars blazed out of a black-velvet sky. No stars in the city. 'S okay by me. He took a deep breath. Go for it, Sonny.

He sprinted away from Jake's little wooden house, his footsteps muffled by the grass, his ponytail slapping against the backpack. Army barbers would chop off the ponytail first thing. Good riddance.

When he reached the road, he glanced back. The house was dark except for the blue glow of Jake's television set. Sonny imagined the old man asleep in his lounge chair. Jake had too many aches and pains to sleep in a bed anymore—he needed to sleep sitting up. Won't miss him.

Won't miss anybody on this raggedy Reservation, especially a crazy old man waiting for the buffalo to come back. Running Braves. If they ever existed at all, they were probably a bunch of bums and alkies. Nobody else ever talked about them.

Never talk to anybody else. Jake off by himself in a corner of the Res with his automobile junkyard and his scrawny dogs; people came by only when they were looking for a car part. Once I quit high school should have just kept going. Anywhere. Shouldn't have promised Mom I'd wait for her to come back for me.

Sonny hitched the pack high on his back and swung into a long, easy stride that would get him to the bus station in Sparta in an hour. He walked down the middle of the unpaved road. No traffic this time of morning. He concentrated on his pace, feeling the muscles of his legs stretch and warm up. He let his arms swing. He enjoyed the dark breeze against his lips and eyelids.

The pain from Hoffer's illegal uppercut was a distant ache. He almost enjoyed feeling it.

Thanks, Furbag, if you hadn't done it, maybe I wouldn't be on the road now, finally getting out of this dump. For good, this time.

For seventeen years, he thought, all my life, she always dragged me back to this sad-sack Reservation when things went wrong for her, and they always did. It was always just for a week that turned into a month, a summer that stretched into a year. Mom would always say, Don't worry, Sonny, this is just a pit stop in the big race, we'll find our own special place real soon, but first I need to nourish my soul, touch the good earth, breathe the clean air, talk to the real people, before we face the world again.

The world always kicked us back to the Res again. Syracuse. Santa Fe. Leave school, leave my friends. Anytime Mom couldn't get her life together, or sell her jewelry, she'd pack us up and head back to the Res. From Brooklyn, Minneapolis, Santa Cruz. Why bother making friends? There was always room at Uncle Jake's—he'd take us in and feed us. And after a while she'd take off again and leave me. Just a few weeks, Sonny, she'd say, give me a few weeks, Sonny, I'll send for you, there's a gallery in SoHo, New York City, loves the earrings.

That was six months ago.

Thinking about his mother dulled his senses. He didn't feel the vibrations under his feet until the truck was bearing down on him, a speeding shadow without headlights. He leaped out of the way. The truck made a screaming half-turn and stopped in a gravel storm.

"Sonny." Jake clambered down stiffly from the cab. He was wearing the tee-shirt and boxer shorts he slept in. His skinny old legs were bean poles in the moonlight. "Where you going?"

"New York. She's gotta sign the papers now."

"She won't do it, Sonny." Jake's voice was tired. "You gonna have to wait till you're eighteen."

"Can't wait."

"You know better, Sonny. She lost her father and brother in the Army, she ain't . . ."

"And my dad. Only Indians count?"

"Wasn't around long enough to count." Jake's false teeth clacked together. That shut him up, thought Sonny. His sore spot. Mom was always his favorite niece, she was everybody's favorite, smart and beautiful and talented, and the first girl off the Res to go to a big-time white college. And then she had to have a baby with a white guy. Every time they look at me, they remember that.

"C'mon back," said Jake.

"I'm going."

"Maybe I been too hard on you, Sonny."

"It's not you, Jake. I got to do this." He suddenly realized he would miss the old man.

"I'll drive you to Sparta."

"I can walk."

"Catch an earlier bus. Be in New York sooner." The old man looked sad.

"Why not?" Sonny unhitched his pack and slung it into the back of the truck. He climbed up into the cab.

They were almost off the Reservation before Jake said, "You think the Army's going to be different?"

"Be different from this."

"Still got to get along with people, follow rules, control yourself."

"I can take care of myself."

"Maybe." The tone in his voice was doubtful. "How's it going to be different from football?"

"Coach didn't like me."

"Didn't like you punching out people."

"Nobody walks over me."

"You take what you got to take till your time comes," said Jake.

"Maybe that's the Redskin way. Not my way."

Jake grunted and turned off the dirt Reservation road onto the paved county highway. They were silent until the lights of Sparta appeared on the horizon. Jake said, "No man ever got to be a Running Brave without taking a dangerous journey. Maybe this is it for you."

"No more old stories, Jake."

"Woods, city, don't matter. Got to survive, get strong as the buffalo, speedy as the deer, wise as the owl. Be a leader for your people."

"Sell it to Hollywood."

They were in Sparta. Jake stopped for the first red light of the trip. He turned to Sonny. "You got to follow the Hawk."

"I'll look him up in the phone book."

"Find the Hawk inside you and let it loose and follow it."

At the green light, Jake turned the corner. A Greyhound was idling at the curb outside the bus station. The driver was loading baggage.

Jake said, "Good luck, Sonny. You can always come back."

"Don't hold your breath." Sonny climbed out of the truck. "Thanks for the ride."

By the time Sonny came out of the station with his ticket, Jake was gone. The driver looked him over, registering the beaded headband, the ponytail, the embroidered denim shirt. His voice was hard. "No booze on my bus."

"Don't have any."

"Then we'll have no problems, boy." He punched the ticket.

The closer to the Res, thought Sonny, the more they hate Indians. For the first hour or so, he knew, no one would want to sit next to him. After that, everybody would want to sit next to an Indian, especially kids. He climbed into the darkened bus and took a window seat in the rear.

He opened his backpack to get his headphones and cassette player. His sketchbook and the box of pencils and charcoals were near the top. He had packed them last, unsure if he really wanted to bring them along.

Leave it, he had thought, it's the old scared Sonny, trapped on the Res, hiding in the back-seats of junkyard cars, drawing birds and leaves and sometimes even Running Braves.

He had finally decided to bring the sketch-book, but throw it away when he got to the city. He didn't want to leave it for someone back there to find and say, Look what goes on in that crazy, half-breed brain.

He slipped a Grateful Dead tape into the player. It had been his dad's favorite music, in college, when he'd met Mom.

Sonny was asleep before the first tape ran out.

3

ONNY STEPPED OFF the bus and the city
smacked him in the face, an explosion of
moving bodies and sudden noise, gusts of
diesel fumes, hot grease, sick flesh. He fought
panic. When you're going into the woods, Jake
always said, first cut a path with your eyes.

He tracked a skinny kid with cinnamon skin
gliding out of a shadow to block his way.

"Welcome to the Apple." He offered a palm
to slap. Sonny glared it away. "Right thing.
Never touch a stranger. You people are wise.
What tribe you from?"

Sonny grunted and kept marching across
the bus terminal, his ponytail slapping time to
the rap of his boots on the marble floor. The kid
skipped alongside in unlaced white sneakers.
Sonny looked him over from a corner of his
eye. He wore a round, brown leather cap on a
boxy bush of orange hair. His body was lost
inside a Free South Africa tee-shirt and plaid

23

Bermuda shorts. He carried a walking stick, a thick, knotted, highly polished club with a steel tip at the bottom and an ivory snake's head on the top. A black leather bag hung from his shoulder. He barely reached Sonny's chin. He could be fourteen years old.

"Never speak to a stranger who could twist your words. Right thing. No wonder you Native American peoples have survived."

"Beat it," growled Sonny. He lengthened his stride to lose the little creep. This may be the woods, but I'm not the hunter here.

"Hey, new face." Sonny whirled into a neon smile. The blond girl had a sweet look under a mask of bright makeup. He slowed to let her keep up. "Don't mind Stick. He thinks he's mayor of the Port."

"Just the welcome wagon, Doll," said the kid.

"How about buying us some breakfast, Mr. Wagon?" Doll winked at Sonny. He felt warm and light-headed. Was it her or the mention of food? He hadn't eaten since before last night's fight. It was nearly four o'clock in the afternoon.

"Ooo-eee," moaned Stick. "You kids are

cold." He put a spidery hand on Sonny's left arm. Before Sonny could shake it off, Doll was hanging on his right sleeve. They steered him through the bus station crowd like expert canoe paddlers avoiding the rocks in the rapids, around lurching beggars, howling kids, sweating tourists. Stick used his snake's-head club to poke people out of their way. Sonny was standing between Stick and Doll at a high table outside a doughnut shop before he figured out how he had gotten there.

"The blueberry, my man, is *numero uno,*" said Stick. He snapped his fingers at Doll. "And let's have some tall and chilly O.J. for the liquids and vitamins necessary in this hellacious weather." He watched Doll hurry off to the counter. "The teen queen likes you. She's usually real shy with strangers."

Sonny slipped off the deerskin pack and dropped it between his feet. He squeezed it with his boot heels. Nobody's going to snatch this and run. Just how dumb you think I am, Weasel? He touched the fat wallet in the back pocket of his jeans. Call Mom again in a few minutes. He had tried the number every time the bus made a rest stop. If there's no answer this time, I'll just go to SoHo, wherever that is. Might as well get some free food first, hear what these hustlers have to say.

"First time in New York?"

"No." He remembered the other times only from the pictures in his pack: his father in uniform, just before he went to Vietnam, holding him in front of a fancy toy store on Fifth Avenue; with his mother's Mohawk cousins in their high-steel hard hats, and posing in front of her jewelry stall at a Brooklyn crafts fair, his little arms hung with necklaces and bracelets.

"N.Y.C. If you can make it here you can make it anywhere," said Stick, waving his club at the crowds surging back and forth across the terminal floor. "And you, my man, could make it here."

"What do you want?" It came out tougher than he had meant it to sound. Too tough. As if he was afraid of Stick.

Stick smiled. Up close, he looked much older than Sonny had first thought. At least eighteen. "Right thing. I knew you were no fool. You could be chief."

"Of what?"

"The street." This time his wave included

the shapes and colors swirling outside the bus station's windows.

"What are you talking about?" He tried not to sound too interested.

"Big, strong, you got a different look. People gonna want a piece of you. Right thing. Long as you get yours."

"Here we go." Doll slid a tray onto the table and served them each a blueberry muffin on a napkin and orange juice in a paper cup. She had bought herself a glazed chocolate dough- nut and a container of coffee.

"I can use you myself," said Stick. "Need a bang-bang."

"That's a security guy," said Doll. She touched his headband. "That's so fresh. What's your name?"

"Sonny."

She offered her hand, warm and damp. "Doll's my street name. It's really Heather, you believe that?" She giggled. Under the powder was a constellation of freckles on her cheeks and nose. She's really younger and softer than she looks, Sonny thought. "You got a place to stay?"

"Yeah." With some luck, I'll be in a barracks

soon, he thought.

"You could own the Deuce," said Stick.

"That's Forty-second Street," said Doll.

"The Deuce, the Doofer," said Stick, "crossroads of the world, the street where the elite meet to beat, cheat and greet sweet meat."

"You can be free on the street," said Doll, "do what you want."

"Right thing," said Stick. "Nobody on your case 24–7–365."

"That's twenty-four hours a day, seven days a week, three hundred and sixty-five days a year," said Doll.

"Chief Sonny knew that," said Stick. "You talk the talk."

Sonny nodded and Doll smiled. Her leg brushed against his under the table. He wondered if it was an accident. She ate very carefully, daintily, little nips off the doughnut, small silent sips of coffee. She blotted a crumb from a corner of her full red lips with a dab of her napkin. She leaned forward and her blouse opened. He could see her soft, freckly, milky-white chest. He wondered how much of the throbbing between his legs was from Hoffer and how much for Doll. Better do what I came to do before I forget what it was.

"Got to make a phone call."

"Be my guest," said Stick. He reached into his black leather bag and pulled out a cellular phone. "Hope you're not calling friends in Tokyo."

"SoHo," said Sonny. He fished the card with his Mom's address and phone number out of his wallet.

Stick flicked a switch and held the phone while Sonny tapped out the number. There was a busy signal. Stick pressed a button. "Memory. It'll keep dialing till it gets through."

Doll said, "SoHo's hot. Art galleries and great clothes. Stick, I told you he was an artist. Aren't you?" Something in her voice made him want to say yes.

"Well, sort of, not really . . ."

"See!" She turned her back to Sonny, her brown eyes bright. They were small eyes, quick, pecking birds' eyes. "I spotted you first."

"True story," said Stick. The phone clicked seven times and growled a busy signal. He set it on the table. "Communications, lifeblood of the modern era."

Dope dealer, thought Sonny. Probably try to sell me some.

"Love art," said Doll. "Believe I used to do

29

clay?" She wiggled her fingers, tipped with black paste-on nails decorated with little stars.

A scarecrow shambled up, shaking a dirty paper cup. "Change?"

Doll wrinkled her nose at the smell, and Stick snapped, "Space!"

The beggar started to speak, took a closer look at the ivory snake head and shuffled off. Sonny was surprised by the hard mask that had slipped over Stick's face.

"The Port can get weird," said Stick. "You need friends, extra eyes. This is a jungle of slimeballs and bonesuckers. Can't trust anybody in the Port or on The Deuce. Especially the pig posse."

"That's cops," explained Doll.

"They think they can do anything 'cause they got the tin."

"Badge," said Doll.

"There is this one pig boss who has dedicated his whole life to busting me," said Stick. He tapped his forehead. "This is one deranged dude."

"Sergeant Alfred Brooks." Doll shook her head. "I'll point him out sometime. Got to watch out for him."

"Maybe he's got to watch out for me," said Stick.

"Maybe later," said Doll. She blinked hard and made a small gesture with her chin.

"Right thing," said Stick. "To be continued, Chief Sonny." He slipped the phone back into the bag. "Bring him by tonight, Doll."

Sonny sensed movement around them, big men, black and white, shoving people out of their way.

Stick scooted into the crowd, hunched over his phone bag, clearing a path with the snake head. He disappeared.

"You'll be okay, Sonny," said Doll. "Just be cool, whatever happens."

The monster fluttered as the men surrounded the table, half a dozen of them in jeans and work shirts. He thought of the bigmouth bozos at the smoker.

One of them said, "Where'd he go, Dolly?"

"He was late for church," she said sweetly.

"Real funny. Take her."

Doll stepped away from the table. One of the men reached out for her. Sonny slapped his arm away.

"Stay out of this, Tonto." Another arm

31

reached out for Doll.

Sonny chopped it down and shoved the man back with a forearm to his chest. Sonny blocked the way as Doll slipped into the crowd.

"Okay, young gentleman, that's enough, it's over." Hands on his shoulders. He glimpsed a dark face behind him.

Sonny pivoted and nailed it with a left, a short crisp hook to the side of a bearded black chin.

As the man crumpled, Sonny saw the badge hanging on a chain around his neck. A cop!

Clubs slammed against his legs and shoulders, one crashed against the back of his head. He went down under a swarm of bodies. It was like football, yeah, just like football, Jake, nobody walks over me, sure, take it till your time comes.

Time out.

4

H E NEVER BLACKED out. He swam through tunnels of darkness and pools of light. He was
jerked to his feet, half carried up stairs,
dumped into a small room that stank of sweat
and smoke. He gagged. A light flashed into his
eyes. A paramedic said, "He'll be okay."

"Redskins are tough." Police officers filled
the room.

"Look what they did to Custer."

"Look what he did to Brooks." The cops
laughed and surrounded him. Half a dozen
hands patted over his body, up his legs. Sonny
reached for his wallet. His back pocket was
torn and empty. The belt loop was torn too. Did
the cops have the wallet? Doll?

"What's your name, Tonto?"

He concentrated on slowing his breathing.
His eyesight was blurred by sweat, but he could
see that the room had no windows. It was bare
except for a table and two chairs and a long

mirror on the wall opposite the door. Too many bodies blocked the way out.

Voices battered him.

"Resisting arrest."

"Striking a police officer."

"You are in deep, Geronimo."

White and black faces hovered in front of him.

"Want to go to jail?"

"Scalp you at both ends in jail."

Sonny's hands curled into fists. Be cool, he told himself, ride it out. But the monster was in his chest.

"So what's your name, where you from?"

The cop's face bobbed into range. A straight right, then the hook. He began to raise his fists. What's the difference between jail and being sent back to the Res?

The door banged open.

A cold, hard voice blew in. "Young gentleman, don't even think about lifting your hands."

Cops scrambled out of the way. A chunky black man swaggered in. He was holding a frosty can of soda to a bearded jaw.

"Put your hands in your pockets, young gentleman, before you mess up your life for good."

Sonny opened his hands and dropped them.

"Leave me alone with this fool."

"Sergeant Brooks, this kid's . . ."

"Pathetic. Leave." He flipped the soda can to one of the cops and waited until they all filed out of the room. He kicked the door shut with his heel. "You are pathetic. Fifteen minutes off the bus and you bought the total New York experience. Saw the whole thing. You let yourself get picked up by two hustlers who ripped off your backpack and wallet. Then you fouled up a drug bust. Must be some kind of a record."

Sonny studied Brooks. He didn't look deranged. He didn't look much of anything. He wasn't particularly tall or heavily muscled. The beginnings of a potbelly pushed out the front of his polo shirt. I could take him out, thought Sonny. Probably has a gun strapped to his ankle under his gray warm-up pants. But one good punch, I could be past him and out the door. Make it to the street. The Deuce. Get to SoHo.

"Tell you how dumb you are, young gentleman. You are thinking right now you could actually get through me." Brooks shook his head. "I am sick of this job and I am tired to death of fools like you." He sighed, closed his eyes and leaned his head against the wall. "Why'd you leave home?"

Sonny shrugged.

"Can't hear you." His eyes were still closed. Sonny wondered if Brooks was daring him to try to escape. "You get thrown out?"

"No."

"Anyone make you do sex?"

"No."

"So why'd you run?"

Sonny grunted.

"Can't hear you. Why?"

"Get away."

"Why?"

It just came out. "Be somebody."

Brooks' eyes opened. "What?"

"Want to be somebody." Sonny wondered, Why am I talking to him?

Brooks straightened up. "Everybody's somebody." His voice wasn't so cold and hard. "Where you from?"

"Upstate."

"How far up which state?"

Sonny shook his head. Answers would land

36

him back on the Res.

"I don't want to put you away. I just want you out of my jurisdiction, on a bus back home. Got that? So what's your name and where you from?"

"Don't matter. I'm here now."

"I'm Sergeant Brooks. I can help you. What's your name?"

Brooks' eyes were warmer than he would have thought. But Sonny shook his head. He wasn't going back to the Res. Got to get to SoHo. Find Mom. Be hard now without the phone number and address.

"You got a real left hook. Ever box?"

Sonny nodded.

"Pro?"

"Not really." Be careful, he thought. Don't get suckered into giving away information. But he wanted to talk to this man.

"How'd you do?" Brooks was smiling. His voice was friendly.

Can't trust anybody in the Port or on The Deuce. Especially the pig posse.

"I asked you, 'How'd you do?'"

The monster whispered, Good enough to clock you, pig.

"Talk to me, young gentleman."

"Good enough to clock you, pig."

Brooks' smile froze. He nodded. "Sound just like Stick. Fine and dandy, young gentleman. You called it." He jerked a thumb at the door. "You're free to go."

"Like that?"

"Like that. Move out before I change my mind."

The cops outside the door eyeballed him all the way to the stairs, but none of them moved. He hurried down the stairs toward the front doors of the bus terminal. He had no idea what to do next. He had no money. But he knew he had to get out of here.

He wasn't ready for the dazzling lights of the street and the roar of traffic. Or the sharp fingernails that dug into his arm.

He cocked his fist and whirled into that neon smile. "Oh, Sonny, you're okay. I was so worried about you."

5

THEY STROLLED THE DEUCE and people checked them out as if they were somebodies. He felt strong and cool with Doll on his arm. He had never before had a girl he was proud to show off, and he swelled with the pleasure of being on parade. She walked tall like she felt it, too.

"Doll!" An older man, maybe forty, bigger than Sonny, his bull neck hung with gold chains, stepped out of a video arcade.

"Later, Mo." Her body tensed and her voice seemed small.

"I need to talk to you."

Doll picked up the pace until they had passed him. "Just some meatball, Sonny, don't mean nothing."

He sensed it meant something, but the street took all his attention. He had never seen anything so filthy and ugly and stinking and full of life.

Rock music pounded out of record stores and fought for airtime with the rap and the salsa blaring from the giant boom boxes. Sidewalk preachers screamed at them to find Jesus before they went to hell. Black men in tee-shirts shook plastic bags: "Hey, rock, reef, loops, cubes." Doll called some of them by name. They nodded and looked Sonny over.

"You hungry? Best pizza in Times Square." She steered him into a narrow little pizza parlor between a movie theater and a souvenir store. Chub's Grotto was just a long counter in front of a wall of ovens and soda spigots. No tables or chairs.

"Listen to this." Doll giggled. "I used to call my dogs back home." She stuck her pinkies into her mouth and made a piercing whistle. "Yo, Chub, any mail or messages for me?"

An enormously fat man wearing only a tomato-stained white apron over his bare upper body waddled down the counter. Tattooed snakes and eagles bit and clawed their way up the mountainous flesh of his arms and shoulders.

"You gonna bust my ears someday, Dolly." He had a high-pitched voice. He leaned over the counter to study Sonny. "Love your outfit."

"My friend Sonny." She squeezed his arm.

"That belt's exquisite," said Chub. "And the headband."

He had forgotten he was still wearing them.

"Sonny's for real," said Doll.

"We're all for real," said Chub. "You thought this was Disney World?"

"I mean he's not just dressed up. He's a real Indian." She looked up at Sonny. "You are, aren't you?"

"Yeah." The farther you get from the Res, the more they love you.

"Apache? Cherokee?" Chub looked serious. "I'm like a Western buff. Read every Louis L'Amour."

"Moscondaga," said Sonny.

"Yeah, right, sure." Chub nodded as if he had heard of the Nation. "Welcome to The Deuce."

"Two slices, pepperoni, extra cheese," said Doll. Chub waddled away. "My treat, Sonny. Stick never has anything to eat at his place 'cause he hardly ever eats."

"You spend a lot of time there?"

"Not if I can help it. He's such a snake." She

wrinkled her nose.

"I thought you were . . ."

"You kidding?" She rolled her eyes in a cute way that flipped Sonny's stomach. "Number-one rule in the Port or on The Deuce, don't trust anybody. Number-two rule. Especially Stick and Brooks."

"Sergeant Brooks wasn't so bad." He wondered why he was defending him.

"Don't let Stick hear you say that."

"Here you go, kids, specialty of the house," said Chub, slapping two limp, greasy triangles on the counter.

He had eaten better pizza in Sparta, but it didn't matter, he was so jacked. The aches and pains were distant now, smothered in excitement. He was out in the real world now, on his own.

"No mail," said Chub, "but I heard that Mo beat up Trini and she split."

"Oh, no," wailed Doll. "She was gonna help me with Jessie."

"Nobody can find her."

"Doesn't she have a sister in Jersey?"

Sonny watched Doll nibble at her slice as daintily as she had eaten her chocolate doughnut at the bus terminal, only an hour ago, before he decked Brooks, before he lost everything he owned. Twelve hours ago he'd been lying in his bunk thinking about the fat farm boy and Jake and Mom, and plotting his escape from the dead zone. And now he was in the middle of everything.

"Mo's going to freak when he finds out Trini split," said Chub.

"He might know already," said Doll. "He says he needs to talk to me."

"You're not going back there?"

"Not if I can get something and pay him back."

Chub's eyes brushed over Sonny. He caught the move. He was somehow already involved in Doll's plans. His skin tingled.

For a while he listened to Doll and Chub gossip about people who were in detox or jail, who had made a score and bought some new clothes, who had tested positive. He lost interest. He watched Chub's assistant, a tiny Asian woman, bustle up and down the counter slapping slices in front of foreign tourists in sandals and shorts, raggedy street kids, junkies, beggars counting coins out of their paper cups, college boys and their dates and a steady stream of hard-eyed black kids his age with beepers on their belts. Crack dealers, figured Sonny. He had seen them on TV. They all frisked him with their eyes. He stared back in the way Jake had taught him to scope strange dogs. Show any fear, they might take a piece out of you just to stay in practice. Show any threat, they'd go for your throat. But eyeball them cool, they won't jump you without good reason. He wished he had Jake's Colt.

Chub was saying, "I could help you take care of Jessie."

"Thanks, but if I didn't have my own place it'd be too risky," said Doll. "One bust, they'd declare me unfit, she'd be in foster and I'd never see her again." She wiped her eyes with the backs of her hands. Her mascara was smeared.

"She is sooo cute," said Chub, stroking Doll's arm.

"I really miss her so much." Doll sniffled.

It sounded as if they were talking about a child. Doll's? She was definitely not older than he was, maybe even younger. Sixteen? The thought that she could be a mother aroused him. He looked at her pale, soft arms. In the neon lights of the pizza parlor the fine hairs on her arms were golden. The spreading warmth pushed away the last twinges of the farm boy's uppercut.

Doll nudged him. When he looked up, startled, she made a small motion with her hand. He turned. One of the beeper dudes was backing out of the store, whispering into his sleeve. When he was out on the street, Chub casually waddled to the door and blocked his view inside.

"Undercover narc," whispered Doll, grabbing his hand. "Follow me."

She pulled him behind the counter and into a tiny bathroom. A door beside the toilet opened into the video arcade. He plunged after her.

The video arcade was jammed, row after row of bodies hunched over muttering, screaming, flashing machines. Bells, horns, squealing brakes, chattering automatic weapons. Sonny felt as though he had entered the guts of a game. He trailed Doll through the room, bouncing off machines and bodies like a pinball. Nobody looked up.

They came to a door. POSITIVELY NO ADMITTANCE. Doll opened it and pulled him into darkness. A red light blinked on. A huge shape loomed up. "Hey, you. . . . Dolly?"

"Trouble, Mo. Get us out back."

Mo bolted the door and led them quickly through a murky corridor of curtained rooms. They reminded Sonny of the dressing cubicles in department stores. He heard moans and sighs. He smelled sweat and ammonia. He glimpsed a man in a suit and a young boy. They reached another door. Mo blocked it and turned to face them.

"What's with this guy."

"He's the one slugged Brooks. We're trying to lose a narc up in Chub's."

"What's that got to do with you?"

"I'm taking him to Stick. That's all there is, Mo."

"You sure, Dolly, this ain't another number?" His voice sounded rough and pleading at the same time.

"Cross my heart. Okay?"

"I got something planned for your birthday."

"That's so sweet, Mo. I got to go. See you tomorrow."

"What time?"

"Eight o'clock."

"You sure?"

"I swear."

"You swear. Watch the steps."

The door closed behind them. Doll took his hand and put it on her shoulder. "Indian file," she said, giggling.

She led Sonny down steps into a storage basement. By the time his eyes adjusted to the darkness, they were through another door and up an iron spiral staircase.

Stick was waiting for them at the top. He was wearing an elegant red-silk robe with a velvet collar. His hair was black now, with a coppery sheen. He looked older, in his twenties.

"Welcome." He ushered them into a dim room. Red bulbs glowed from the corners. Sonny felt a thick rug underfoot. A gentle waterfall of music poured out of overhead speakers. Incense. Doll guided him to a soft couch. As he sank into the cushions, he realized how tired he was.

"Some layout, huh?" said Doll. "Who'd believe this under The Deuce?"

"You can stay here tonight, Chief Sonny,"

said Stick. "I owe you one. Brooks was after me and you got in the way."

"I owe him one, too," said Doll. She sat down next to Sonny and rested her head on his shoulder. "How about giving Sonny a run?"

"This is no training program," said Stick. "I need experienced people."

"You need people you can trust," said Doll.

"You want to make some change?" asked Stick.

Sonny tried to sound tough and casual. "What's the deal?"

"Delivery. To New Jersey."

"Won't they be looking for him?" asked Doll.

"Sure. But they won't touch him," said Stick. "Brooks let Sonny go as a decoy. He'll never bust Sonny as long as I'm loose. He figures Sonny will lead him to me."

"How do you know that?" asked Sonny.

"I'm in that pig's head. It's him against me for the Port."

"You really hate him so much," said Doll.

"He's a hypocrite. The world is setting up for the final war between the colored races and the white slave masters, and I hate any man of color who lines up with the enemy."

"Stick's real political," said Doll. She sounded proud of him.

"We're just the little retailers in this drug thing, Sonny. The white man makes the serious money. He's got those foreign dictators to grow it, ship it here. When you got a black cop coming down on the brothers, that is hypocrisy."

Stick picked up his walking stick. "Someday I'll give Brooks a bite of the snake. I don't think he knows I'm strapped."

"Packed," said Doll. "Carrying a gun."

"That's a gun?" asked Sonny.

"Bottom's a pig sticker." Stick pulled off the steel tip to expose a dagger. "Top's a shotgun." He pulled off the ivory snake's head to expose a barrel. "A load of buckshot can cut a man in half."

Doll shuddered. "Put that away."

Stick snapped the tip and head back onto the stick and dropped it behind the couch. "Back to business."

"You really think it's safe for Sonny to make a run?" Her leg was pressed against his.

"Brooks won't touch him."

"Okay," said Doll, "how much?"

"You his agent?" Stick sounded annoyed.

49

"I'm his friend."

"Top dollar. A Benjy."

"That's a hundred," explained Doll. "Benjamin Franklin's on the hundred-dollar bill." She turned back to Stick. "Double or nothing."

"He's a rookie."

"He's strong and smart."

"He's never made this kind of bread. Have you?"

"Sure," said Sonny. "Boxing."

Doll squealed. "You were a pro boxer?"

"Sort of. Smokers upstate. We got paid."

Stick looked interested. "You thinking about fighting in the city?"

"Maybe." He hadn't really thought about it until he heard the interest in Doll's voice.

"I could get behind a boxer," said Stick. "Wouldn't mind a piece of the next Mikey T. How'd you do?"

"Won five in a row." Hoffer doesn't count, he thought.

"Right thing."

"One thing at a time," said Doll. "Two hundred or nothing."

"You taking a commission?" asked Stick.

Her voice was coy. "Maybe he'll take me out on my birthday."

Sonny wished he could see her face. "When's that?"

"Next Thursday."

"How old you going to be?"

"I'll tell you then." Her leg was pressing harder.

"We'll do details in the morning," said Stick, "but here's your contract." He tore a hundred-dollar bill in half, handed one piece to Sonny and waved the other. "You get this and the other hundred when you get back." His voice turned sarcastic. "If that's okay with your agent."

"For now. But our price goes up after this one. Sonny needs to get some rest." She knelt in front of him and pulled off his boots. "These real cowboy boots?"

"They were made for me in New Mexico."

"You've been there? I've never been anywhere. Maybe you'll take me someday." She lifted his legs onto the couch and arranged a pillow under his head as Stick snapped off the red lights.

She kissed Sonny's forehead. He reached for her. She slipped out of his arms. "When you get back," she said.

6

SONNY STRODE THE DEUCE, trying to look cooler than he felt. A cheap nylon gym bag dangled casually from his right hand as if it held nothing more valuable than workout clothes. But the gym bag's straps were tightly wound around his wrist. No way someone could snatch it. As if anyone on Forty-second Street this morning seemed capable of a rip and run.

The Deuce looked hung over, as tired and groggy as he had felt when Stick had prodded him awake with the metal tip of his club, the pig-sticker end. It took Sonny a moment to remember where he was. Even after two cups of coffee he had to repeat Stick's instructions aloud to remember them. A bus to Camden, New Jersey, where he would be met by a black kid wearing a Malcolm X tee-shirt who would ask him what time it was. Sonny would say, "The time's now." The kid would say, "That's the right time." Sonny would follow him into the bathroom and trade his gym bag for a black leather shoulder bag. Sonny would take the next bus back to New York and go straight to Chub's to wait for Doll.

At the mention of her name, Doll staggered out of another room, rubbing her eyes.

Without makeup, the freckles dark on her pale skin, she looked fourteen. Her brown eyes were bloodshot. He wondered where she had slept. She could barely talk. She wiped her runny nose. He wondered if she had taken drugs.

"You clear?" asked Stick. When he nodded, Stick handed him a round-trip bus ticket and a five-dollar bill. "Showtime. Don't miss your bus," and he pushed him out the door.

He made his way down the iron spiral staircase and through the corridor of cubicles and into the video arcade and out onto The Deuce.

Few hustlers were on the street yet. Sonny moved against a tide of suburban commuters hurrying out of the Port. Stay cool, slow your heart, make your face a mask, cut a path with your eyes. Inside the Port he checked the stairway to the long-distance gates before he started down. A few beggars, a few commuters, no one who looked out to get him.

Was Stick right? Had Brooks let him go as a decoy? Was he safe from arrest as long as Stick was loose?

He didn't feel safer. Just meant that Brooks was another person trying to use him.

He spent most of the five dollars on orange juice, coffee and two doughnuts for the bus ride. The driver took his ticket without looking up. The bus was nearly empty. He sat near the back, alongside an emergency exit. He kept the gym bag on his lap.

A few more passengers climbed aboard. In the dim light he couldn't make them out. A black couple sat down behind him. Their faces were hidden by the brims of big hats. A white couple in jeans and matching sweatshirts sat in front of him. All the room in this bus and everybody crowds around me.

Don't get paranoid, Sonny. Maybe they just like Indians in New York.

The couple in front began to neck. Sonny relaxed. Piece of cake. Just kick back and daydream about spending two hundred bucks on a hot girl who likes me. He drank the juice. It cleared a cool, sweet channel from his throat to his belly.

The driver swung aboard and counted passengers, then sat down and gunned his engine. A few more minutes and we'll be on the road, heading south, starting my new life. Free. On my own. For the first time, doing what I want to do, making my own choices. No more being dragged to powwows, made to dress up to sell jewelry, no more being dumped on the Res when life goes wrong, no more fighting smokers for a crazy old man who lives in the past.

Here comes Sonny Bear, Chief of The Deuce.

The driver closed the door and kept gunning the engine, but the bus wasn't moving. Sonny glanced out the window. Drifting shapes alongside the bus. Beggars and commuters. But even the beggars looked big and healthy.

The hair on the back of his neck itched. They're just dressed like beggars and commuters.

He watched a police car glide alongside the bus.

Sonny yanked the iron lever of the emergency exit. He had the door half open when the white couple in front of him came out of their clinch and lunged over the back of their seat.

The woman shoved the barrel of a gun into his nose. "Police, you're under arrest."

Behind him, a familiar voice said, "Ah, New Jersey. Were you planning an educational tour of the Garden State, young gentleman?"

7

"YOU ARE OBVIOUSLY determined to screw yourself into an early grave," said Brooks. He sounded disgusted. "Too bad. A left hook is a terrible thing to waste."

Sonny's hands were cuffed behind his back to a hard plastic chair in the small room with the long mirror. He faced Brooks across the little white table.

"You know you were carrying crack?" asked Brooks.

Sonny stared at the wall. If he said, Yes, he'd be guilty. If he said, No, he'd sound like a fool.

"Mules," said Brooks. "The street word for delivery boys like you. Mule is a cross between a horse and a jackass. No brains, no future. Good for nothing but to carry."

Brooks stood up and turned away. He wore his gun under his belt against the small of his back. It was a big shiny silver automatic.

"You have any idea what crack is doing to this city, this country?" Brooks talked to the wall in a flat, cold voice. "How many people are dead? Not just users and mules and dealers, but little kids who got caught in a crossfire. Mushrooms. That's what they call innocent bystanders. Mushrooms."

He turned slowly and faced Sonny. "Stick's part of an uptown dope posse, call themselves X-Men. Pretend they're some kind of African-American heroes. They ship crack to middle schools in New Jersey." His face seemed darker, his eyes were slits. "Poison eleven-year-olds. You want to be part of that?"

Sonny couldn't look Brooks in the eyes.

"They plucked you off the bus like a chicken, made you think you had friends in the Apple. Doll got you all hot and bothered, right? It's their M.O. You're not the first." Sonny felt the heat rise up his neck and redden his face. "And now you're ready to take a fall for two people who gave you half a counterfeit hundred." He laughed, a harsh, snorting sound.

"You are on your way to the slam, young gentleman. Felony time. For what?" Brooks sat down and leaned across the table. His face was so close, Sonny could see the tiny beads of sweat glistening between the sharp black hairs of his mustache and beard. "All I need is your statement. Everything that happened since you hit town yesterday. And then I can turn you right around with a bus ticket out of this mess. It's Stick I want, not you."

Sonny stared at the wall, struggling to control his breathing, to swallow down the fear rising in his throat. I may be a mule, but I'm not a rat.

"Let me tell you what's going to happen," said Brooks. "Some poor, overworked public defender will do the best she can for you, which won't be much. Meanwhile, the district attorney's going to want high bail because you're from out of town. The way the courts are backed up, you could rot for weeks, months, before your trial. In a hole with some heavy-duty psychos."

"I can take care of myself," said Sonny.

"You're tough, you got pride," said Brooks. "I can get behind that. But for crack? Stick sells death to kids. How you justify that?"

Brooks was staring at him so intently, he felt he had to answer, but all he could do was shrug. He had no answer. He had never thought about it until now. Mules and mushrooms and selling death to kids.

"Pushers reel in the kids like fish on a hook, listen to them scream for more, they'll do anything for dope, lie, cheat, whore, rob, kill. You want a piece of that?" His voice rose, his chunky body quivered. "Give me Stick and you walk."

Brooks stood up and came around the table. "What you say?" His polo shirt was dark with sweat. "I'm giving you a chance to go home."

Sonny lowered his head. He tried to sort the feelings running through his body and the thoughts jumbled in his mind. Stick was just using him. Okay. But what about Doll? If he turned in Stick, would she go to jail, too? He couldn't narc on her.

And a chance to go home. What did that mean?

"Look at me." Brooks pulled his ponytail, jerking his head back up. "You gonna be a dumb mule all your life?"

Sonny stared into Brooks' face. The beads of water hung on the bristly tips of his mustache and beard, and pooled in the hollows under his eyes. "I don't know what makes me crazier, a piece of garbage like Stick or a kid like you who could be somebody if he tried. You ever stay with anything long enough to find out if you could do it?"

The monster clawed up his legs.

"What happened with your boxing? Too many rules? Didn't want to spend the time finding out if you were really good or not? Afraid to find out? Just wanted to throw the big hook?"

He felt his own eyes narrow as he glared at Brooks.

"That woke you up. Okay, hotshot, let's see what you got." Brooks was behind him, unlocking the handcuffs. "Stand up."

His right wrist was still cuffed to the chair, but his left arm was free. He stood up. He was a head taller than Brooks. He could see the beginnings of a bald spot on the top of Brooks' head. The monster filled him.

"Go ahead, throw that big left hook."

Sonny didn't set his feet, he just fired a quick one at the bearded chin, a sucker punch that should have smashed the grinning black face against the wall. But Brooks casually tilted his head, and the punch missed by inches.

"Got to do better than that, young gentleman."

Another one, angled down, but Brooks leaned away at the last instant and Sonny staggered off balance. The plastic chair banged against his leg.

"Dynamite hook, but it's not enough."

Sonny feinted, then threw a long hook, but Brooks was moving, small dance steps that took him out of range. He must have been a boxer once, thought Sonny.

"Rules, discipline, can't run away from that."

Shut up, he thought, hurling himself behind a roundhouse left. Brooks ducked under it.

"Can't run away from anything."

He threw three in a row, bangers, but they struck air and the plastic chair whacked his shoulder and the back of his head. The anger in his chest filled his throat. He hooked and missed again. His shoulder ached. He tried to blink the sweat out of his eyes.

"Your hook could be heavyweight champ." Brooks skipped to the center of the room. His arms dangled at his sides, mocking Sonny. "But the rest of you is chump of the world."

Sonny lunged forward, but his arm was tired, his legs were wobbly, all he had now was the monster and it wasn't enough. He was pushing his punches, staggering after Brooks, dizzy in the heat of the little room. The bearded face was always just out of range, taunting him.

Sonny's throat closed down. Air. The monster asked, You going to take this? Fight him one-handed? You are a dumb mule if you let him make the rules for you. Sonny's right hand closed around the top of the hard plastic chair. It was heavier than he thought, but he swung it over his head and hurled himself at Brooks, slam the chair into that sneering black face, crush it, but Brooks whirled away and Sonny smashed into the wall and slid to his knees, retching and gasping for air.

"Tell me about Stick," said Brooks. "Everything. What he said. What he did. Where he squats. What you saw and heard. From jump, yesterday at the bus."

Sonny shook his head.

"Go on. From the beginning." Brooks grabbed his ponytail and pulled his head back.

"No."

"FROM THE BEGINNING." His voice thundered in the little room.

"No."

Brooks yanked on the ponytail. Sonny's eyes bulged; he gasped for air.

The door burst open, the room was filled with blue uniforms. "Easy, Sarge." Brooks let go. Sonny slumped to the floor.

"Call a wagon," said Brooks wearily. "Bury the fool."

8

H E WAS HELPLESS, a child again, his life out of his control. He was searched, stripped of his headband and belt and boots, fingerprinted, photographed, talked at by guards, judges, lawyers. He was pushed into vans and dragged through courthouses, chained by the ankle to other prisoners. He didn't eat so he wouldn't have to use the stinking toilet holes in cells jammed with bodies that reeked of booze, vomit, feces. He kept his back against a wall and his face hard and tried not to sleep. The other prisoners left him alone. In the dark he heard them struggle with each other in thrashing, whimpering mounds. He kept his mouth shut and his hands ready. The monster was silent.

His lawyer was a thin, jittery, dark-haired woman who snapped chewing gum as she talked. She opened a brown folder. "George Harrison Bayer, last known address Moscondaga Reservation."

He must have looked surprised, because she said, "The belt said Sweet Bear Crafts, an easy trace. Listen, they want to make a deal. Tell Brooks about Stick and I can get you off."

He shook his head.

"Well, think about it, George. I gotta go."

He saw Brooks at one of his hearings, standing in a corner, arms crossed, staring at him as Sonny's lawyer argued with the assistant district attorney. She was another skinny white woman with dark hair and a sharp voice. The judge was a large black man who looked bored.

Sonny's lawyer said, Here's a naïve hick from a poverty-stricken reservation who's been victimized in the big city. Given the way Native Americans have been exploited in this country, how about giving this kid a break.

The D.A. said, That's silly, everyone in America knows about crack, no ethnic group is any less responsible for its actions than any other.

Sonny's lawyer said, At least let him go without bail so he can go home or into a runaway shelter in the city.

The D.A. said, No way, he would just run again, and besides, the police gave him a

66

chance to cooperate in the battle against drugs and he refused.

Sonny's lawyer said, Send him to Whitmore and he'll become a hardened criminal.

The D.A. said, Turn him loose, it's a message to every red, white, black, yellow and brown kid that the Law plays favorites.

The judge said, No people has a franchise on good or bad or responsibility or lack of it. George H. Bayer. Whitmore. Next.

When it was over, the D.A. shook hands with Brooks.

Sonny was shoved into a van with three other teenaged boys and driven north. He knew the direction because they crossed the Hudson River and kept the water on their right for almost an hour. The three spoke in Spanish. The one who did the most talking had a tattoo on the back of his left hand, a flower and a dagger crossed. It looked as though it had been drawn with a sewing needle and ink. The tough kids on the Res would come back from jail with homemade tattoos. The boys in the van kept glancing at Sonny. He sensed they were talking about him.

The van drove under a huge sign WHITMORE HILLS JUVENILE CORRECTIONAL FACILITY and into the center of a cluster of gray-green barracks surrounded by a tall barbed-wire fence. They were unloaded on a dusty ballfield.

"New boys, let's go, new boys." A cocky little man in a gray uniform herded them toward a barracks door marked RECEPTION CENTER. "Hard time, easy time, you do the time or the time does you. I'm Lieutenant Deeks, and if you cross me once, I'll put some hurt on you. Cross me twice and I'll cross you out."

In a barracks shower room they were stripped and hosed down by other prisoners who laughed at them shivering in the cold water. They were splashed with disinfectant and anti-louse shampoo. They dried off with towels the size of handkerchiefs. They were issued tee-shirts, shower clogs and drawstring sweatpants. Everything was stamped W.H.J.C.F.

They were marched into a room with a barber chair. One of the Spanish kids cursed as a woman in civilian clothes hacked off his long black hair.

"Next," she said to Sonny.

He shook his head. He was going to keep his hair. It was all he had left.

"Deeks," she called.

The little lieutenant ran in. "What going on?"

The barber pointed her clippers at Sonny.

"You crossing me," he glanced at his clipboard, "Mr. George H. Bayer?"

"I am Sonny Bear, a member of the Moscondaga Nation. This is how we wear our hair."

"I don't care if you are Sitting Bull," said Deeks. He rocked on the balls of his spit-shined black shoes. "Whitmore rules. It's no hair, so get in the chair, Mister Bayer." He laughed and winked at the barber, who rolled her eyes.

The monster filled his belly and curled his hands into fists.

"Let's go, Tonto. Get 'em up, Scout. Into the chair, kemo sabe." He was enjoying himself.

The barber cleared her throat. "You might want to check this, Lieutenant. That civil liberties case we had last . . ."

"That was religious," said Deeks. He was rocking faster now and a red flush inched up his neck. "Injun ponytails don't mean dip. Into the chair, Little Beaver—I am losing patience."

Crush this bug, said the monster. "The way I wear my hair is a symbol of . . ."

"Into the chair," snarled Deeks. "I don't even know if you're really Indian, you don't look that Indian, you ain't that dark, your face ain't flat, you could be some kind of Eye-talian, you don't have a Indian name, you could be anything, try to pull something on me, I've had enough." He pulled a blackjack out of his back pocket. "Into the chair." He poked the lead tip into Sonny's belly. "Let's go, let's go now . . . hey!"

Deeks was tough. The first punch turned his head and buckled his knees but didn't put him down. He tried to raise the blackjack.

The second left hook knocked him flat.

9

H E WAS DUMPED into a sealed iron box without a window. The toilet was a smelly hole in the floor next to the bed, which was a rotting mattress. He couldn't tell if it was day or night. Even the prison sounds, the bells and whistles and clanging doors, were distant and muffled. Meals were shoved through a slot at the bottom of the door. They were always the same—a cup of weak, lukewarm coffee and a sandwich of greasy-green bologna on stale white bread. He never saw the guard's hands.

He remembered Jake's stories about the final test of a Running Brave, the solo on Stonebird, the highest mountaintop on the Reservation, days and nights of surviving off the land and wrestling with the question:

Do I really want to be a Running Brave?

A courier, a diplomat, a warrior, a peace bringer, always on call to the Nation, always in training, to run a hundred miles, to sit a hundred hours, to fight to the finish, to speak with wisdom.

He shook his head to clear it. Why am I trancing out on the bedtime stories of a misfit Moscondaga?

And why am I crouched in the corner of this cell like I used to be in the backseats of Jake's junkyard wrecks, hiding from the world and drawing weird pictures?

He sketched on the white Styrofoam trays from his meals, using the plastic tip of his sweatpants drawstring as a pen. For ink, he moistened the dark grime on the cell floor with spit.

He drew Doll and Mom.

He remembered how he would see things in a face he was drawing that he never saw when he was looking at it in the flesh. Doll's eyes, quick and pecking, the eyes of a bird poised either to fly away or to swoop down on a morsel of food, were just like Mom's eyes. Always looking for something, just over your shoulder, around the corner, in the next town.

He drew Doll's body as he imagined it, full and firm. He thought of them together. On her birthday. He would have taken her to dinner and to a club with his money from Stick. Was the Benjy really counterfeit? And if it was, did Doll know it? He didn't want to believe she did. He concentrated on drawing her hair.

The door clanged open. A guard said, "You got five minutes, Sergeant."

"Solitary confinement." The door clanged shut. "You are so predictable, young gentleman."

He was glad to see Brooks, but all he could say was "What do you want?"

"D.A. won't lower your bail, and Jake Stump can't raise it."

"You talked to Jake?"

"I don't have much time." He spoke softly and quickly. "We've arranged for you to be released into the general population. First thing, the posses'll try to recruit you. I want you to join X-Men."

"Why?"

"You won't have to do anything, not even the tattoo. Tell 'em it's against your culture. Like the hair bit." He snorted.

"You think I made that up?"

"I don't care. Now, listen. X-Men don't want you joining the Latin Knights or staying independent—looks like you're facing them. So go along, hang with them a couple of weeks. You do that, tell me what you hear, then I can go to the D.A. and get the bail dropped and get you out of here."

Just another way to get at Stick, Sonny thought. Stick deserved to be in jail if he was selling death to kids. If you believed what Brooks said. But what about Doll? Would she go to jail, too? She had a baby somewhere.

"I don't know."

There was a knock on the door. "Minute, Sarge."

"You got to do it." There was desperation in his voice. "We can bust these animals."

"I can't narc for you."

Brooks took a deep breath. "You ever wonder how I knew you were on that bus?"

"You followed me."

"Don't have enough officers for that. You were a decoy. Stick let us know about you through one of our undercovers he'd made. We went after you while Stick sent out a major shipment with somebody else."

Brooks' voice was bitter. "He must of laughed his skinny little butt off at me. And at you. Didn't you learn not to trust anybody on The Deuce?"

The door opened. "Gotta go, Sarge."

Sonny said, "Can't trust you either."

Brooks squeezed the bridge of his nose. "You don't have much choice right now." He walked out. "It's a done deal."

The guard beckoned Sonny. "Let's go, chief."

Sunlight slapped his face, closed his eyes. He stumbled, blinking, into the dusty yard. Hundreds of young men milled, smoking, playing volleyball and basketball, lifting weights, soaking up rays.

Someone shouted, "Sonny Bear!"

They began to clap, a rhythmic pounding that slowly built into rolls of thunder as the games stopped, and they all turned to him and began chanting, "Son-nee, Son-nee, Son-nee . . ."

The loudspeaker crackled, "There will be no demonstrations, repeat, there will be no demonstrations. . . ."

The chanting and clapping subsided gradually. There were boos.

"Nobody liked Deeks," said the guard who

had brought him out. "You're a hero. God help you."

At dinner he was passed up to the head of the chow line. The food servers behind the steam table winked and dumped extra portions on his tray. His table was crowded.

"Deeks is history, man."

"Some liberties lawyer call from the city, heard what happen, say they sue for your rights, man, if they don't let you out."

Was that the cover story, or had Brooks arranged that to happen?

"What you hit him with, Sonny?"

"You gonna turn pro, Sonny?"

"Let the man eat, fool."

"Tomorrow, Sonny, when you see the shrink, tell her you got claus-tro-pho-bi-a, got to get a outside job."

"That dumb. He want the kitchen."

"So he be fat, like you?"

"Fool, he can't get no job till he be sentenced."

He let the conversation wash over him. The kids who clustered around him were the smaller, younger ones, looking for a protector, too weak to worry about appearing weak. The rabbits and the small deer of the forest.

"So what kind of Indian you be?"

"Moscondaga."

"That is cool."

There were others, who watched from a distance, measuring him. The wolves and the mountain lions.

"They gon' make you choose, Sonny. X-Men or Latin Knights. What you gon' do?"

Just before lights-out, he was assigned a top bunk in a barracks room with twenty bunk beds on each side. After the silence of solitary, the breathing of eighty bodies was a hurricane of whistles and snores and sobs. A guard and an inmate clomped through the barracks shining a flashlight into each bunk, checking off a list on a clipboard. Bed check.

He waited until the hurricane settled into a steady moan in the dark before he slipped down from the bunk and padded across the wooden floor to the latrine. He blinked in the bright light. It was empty. He went to the farthest toilet before he pulled the piece of Styrofoam tray from under his shirt. Doll stared back at him.

She was going to like this. With the sharpened point of his plastic drawstring tip dipped in blood from his earlobe, he would draw a beautiful red dress to cover her nakedness. It would be her birthday card.

He heard shuffling feet, heavy breathing.

There were five of them, huge and blue-black against the bright, white tiles. They stood in formation, four of them shoulder to shoulder, feet spread, wrists crossed, a tattooed X on the back of each right hand.

The fifth, the leader, stood in front of them.

"Welcome to Whitmore, Brother Sonny." He extended his hand. It was limp. "I am X-One. We respect a man of color who stands up for what's right." His voice had a flat, robot quality. "X-Men are freedom fighters. You may join us."

"I am a member of the Moscondaga Nation. I answer only to the Clan Mothers and the Chiefs." He enjoyed the sudden flare of old X's nostrils. He wasn't used to being talked to like this.

"In Whitmore," snapped X-One, "you answer to posse X."

The four X-Men behind him snapped into a martial-arts ready position. The monster chuckled and flexed. Fire the hook, Sonny, make X an ex.

Maybe you just can't go through life popping the hook, then letting whatever happens to you happen to you. Maybe you got to make a plan.

The plan is, Mash the dude.

"Posse sounds like a bunch of white men riding after my people."

My people. You want it both ways, white and red. Why not? I got stuck with it both ways.

"I understand," said X-One. "As a Indian, you don't trust nobody, which is cool. But the black and the red peoples is united here." His voice echoed against the white latrine walls. "X-Men are your brothers."

"My brothers are the warriors of the Moscondaga. You're buffalo chips to me."

Sonny watched the X-Men shift, glance at one another. X-One was thrown off stride, he looked confused.

Makes two of us, thought Sonny.

Brooks said I was predictable. He had me figured. Figured I'd mule for Stick, figured I'd punch out Deeks. Now what?

Did he figure the big dumb Indian would

join X-Men and narc for him, or did he figure I'd wipe these boxheads out?

Maybe I'm not going to do either one. Figure that, Brooks.

X-One scowled. "What's funny?"

Sonny turned and walked away. His bare feet slapped on the tile floor. The hairs on the back of his neck tingled.

"You don't got no choice." X-One's voice was shrill. "You don't dis X-Men."

He thought he was going to make it. He was almost at the latrine door when they hit him, two on his back like wolves on a deer. He smashed one of them up against the wall, then stiffened with a sharp pain in his back. Another sharp pain in his side. Something heavy hit the back of his head.

He fell. He felt the Styrofoam birthday card crunch under his chest. The cool tiles soothed his hot cheek. Before his eyes dimmed out, he saw his blood spill across the white floor. The color of Doll's dress.

10

SONNY DREAMS he is walking the wind.

Below him, beneath the clouds, are the purple-green hills of Moscondaga.

A man moves swiftly up a trail, along a ridge, down a hill. He is a courier for the Nation. A Running Brave. He disappears around a switchback, reappears. Jake Stump. His face is scarred by his years, but his body is young and limber. He is carrying a message. "'S okay, boy, you gonna be okay." His voice, soft and steady, is brought to Sonny on the wings of a hawk.

There are two runners on the trail now, matching strides along the valley floor. The sun glints off the gun tucked against the small of Al Brooks' back. "Young gentleman, you're going to be fine."

"Can't make him stay on the Res," said Jake.

"He's dead meat loose in this city," said Brooks.

Plastic bags swayed above Sonny. Tubes snaked out of them into his arms.

"Find his mother," said Jake. "Maybe she'll sign now."

"Won't matter. Army won't touch him till his indictment's dropped."

"How long?"

"Who knows? Courts are jammed."

The voices drift away.

He follows them out to The Deuce where Doll is waiting. She wears beaded white buckskin. "Where've you been, Sonny boy?" Behind her, in the Grotto, Mo throws pizza dough.

Sonny reaches for Doll, but up close the face is his mother's. "Where've you been?"

"Getting something going for us, Sonny. Mo really likes my rings and earrings—he's going to sell them in his arcade." Mom's bird eyes peck at him. "I'll make a bundle. I'll send for you. We'll have a tepee of our own."

He awoke to searing pain, to his own screams.

"Nurse!" shouted Brooks.

A pinprick high on his arm, and he walks the wind again.

Below, they run the trails and talk.

"Sonny hits you right," said Jake, "you get up reeeal slow."

"Tell me about it. Some left hand."

"The best. And quick. But he won't listen."

Sonny felt warm and safe, as if they were carrying him along the trail between them.

"You been training him?" asked Brooks.

"Some. Had him down to a gym in Sparta. Did real good for a while. Then some jerk started giving him a hard time and Sonny wiped the floor with him."

"Short fuse," said Brooks.

"Nope. Always been a real quiet kid, don't say much, sneaks off to draw pictures, nobody supposed to know about that, and he lets himself get pushed around. Then, all of a sudden, look out."

"Passive-aggressive personality," said Brooks.

"Evil spirit," said Jake.

"You believe that?"

"Ever see *The Exorcist*? Like that, only an Indian spirit. Got to come out or it eats you up inside, destroys you. Once it comes out, it's a hawk you can follow where you need to go."

"A hawk," said Brooks. "Gimme a break."

"While it's inside, make you crazy. Like what happened with that guard."

"That wasn't crazy—it was logical. To save his hair."

"Never cared about that before. Favored his white side."

"White side?"

"Father was a white man. Killed in Vietnam. So they say."

Sonny tried to move closer to their voices. They were talking about his father. His mother always changed the subject when he asked about his father.

The doctor pinched his big toe. "You were lucky, son. The tip of the knife was a millimeter from your heart."

Jake snorted. "Lucky wouldn't of got cut a-tall."

The doctor chuckled politely. "So, you ready to get up and walk for me?"

Two nurses swung his legs over the side of the bed. They had to lift him and support him. His legs couldn't bear the weight.

The pain amazed him, a scalding tidal wave. He gasped and lost his breath. The hospital gown was soaked with sweat and spotted with blood leaking out from the stitches that ran along his back and side.

"That's it, that's it," cheered the nurses.

"Go, boy," said Jake.

The doctor said, "Another step for me now, Sonny."

He did it for Brooks, who sat silent and stony faced in a corner, staring at him, willing him on. He wanted to stop, to sink back into bed, to get a shot that would send him painlessly back to the clouds, but Brooks' stare was pushing him one shuffling step after another with a nurse's shoulder under each armpit like a crutch, the bags of intravenous solution swinging overhead from the metal pipe rack. Keep going, young gentleman, show me there's more to you than just hit and run.

"Attaboy," said Jake.

"Way to go," cheered the nurses.

The doctor was talking to Brooks. "Strong kid. He beat the infection. Now we have to reverse muscle atrophy and the loss of lung and gut function. Ten days is a long time to be on your back."

Ten days, thought Sonny. It seemed like hours.

"He should be running in another ten days," said Brooks.

"Well, uh—" the doctor stroked his chin— "have to see how he progresses, um, talk about discharging him in a week or . . ."

"Be out of here by Friday," said Brooks. "Jake'll have him on the road the following Monday. Easy mile to start."

"Isn't he still technically, er, a prisoner?" asked the doctor.

"Don't sweat it, Doc," said Brooks. "He is my prisoner."

He got a cute get-well card, a cartoon cat hanging by the tips of its claws from a rope held over a cliff by a grinning mouse. Inside was the printed line "Hang in there," and, written in a childish scrawl, "To Sonny, All My Love, Heather." There was no return address.

When the nurses came to take him walking in the corridor, one of them taped the card to the wall of his bed and kidded him about his girlfriend. He felt good. He worked hard that morning, driving himself to extra laps around the nurses' stations. When he got back, he pulled down the card and hid it. Brooks might know that Heather was Doll's real name.

Brooks looked too tired to notice anything when he arrived after dinner. He flopped into a chair by the bed. "Stakeouts kill you."

"Stick?"

"I'll get him."

"You really hate him."

"Long story."

"I'm not going anywhere tonight."

"I'll make it short. James Mosely was my best friend—we did everything together from kindergarten, stayed with me when my mother . . . anyway, he got in with a bad crowd, started shooting heroin. I helped him get clean. We joined the airborne together, must of saved each other's life a dozen times in Nam. Got back home, they were waiting for him with the first free fix. Month later, he OD'ed. Every time I think about Stick, I think about James, all those Jameses still out there. . . ."

Brooks wiped his eyes and left the room. It took Sonny a long time to fall asleep that night. He had never had a friend like James. To see him die after all they went through together. From drugs. Sold by someone like Stick.

*   *   *

One night, as they watched a prizefight on TV, Brooks bobbed his head to the punches.

"You box?" asked Jake.

"A little amateur, when I was his age."

"You any good?" asked Sonny.

"Quick enough. But no killer instinct, no big punch."

"How'd you get started?" asked Sonny.

"I was going nowhere, neighborhood gang was giving me grief, so I went to learn to fight. Man's dead now, but his gym is still there. Donatelli's Gym, right on Hundred-twenty-fifth Street and Seventh Avenue in Harlem. Friend of mine, Henry Johnson, runs it now. After Jake gets you in shape, you'll train there."

Jake was nodding. "Al's got a plan."

"You do want to be a fighter, don't you?" asked Brooks.

Sonny pushed himself higher in the bed. "I don't know."

"Never know anything till you try." Brooks pointed up at the screen. "You think those guys are better than you?"

Two blurry shapes on the black-and-white set hanging from the ceiling pounded each other in quick flurries that left them panting.

Sonny weighed his answer. He wanted to please Brooks. Finally, he said, "No."

"Wrong," said Brooks. "You might have a better punch, you might even be quicker and smarter and stronger, but they got off their butts and did it, ran every day, put in hours at the gym, cut out booze and junk food, watched films of old fights, listened to their trainers."

"I could do that," said Sonny.

"They got control of themselves."

"I could try."

Brooks said, "We'll see."

There was a party the night before he was discharged. The doctors, nurses, some of the other patients on the floor, crowded in to eat the cake, ice cream, soda, chips, that Brooks brought. "Enjoy it while you can," said Brooks. "Once you're in training, you can forget this stuff."

Mrs. Brooks showed up, a round-faced woman with an easy smile. Sonny had never thought of Brooks as being married, of having a life outside the Port. When Mrs. Brooks showed him pictures of their two little daughters, he felt jealous.

Jake had news about Mom. "She ain't been in the city for a while, but this art gallery sold some stuff for her and they say she'll be checking in soon. Left a message for her to call us at the Res."

He hoped she wouldn't call. Brooks had a plan for him. She could only spoil it.

On his way out, Brooks squeezed his shoulder. It was the first friendly physical gesture he had ever made. "You listen to Jake now. He can get you strong. Those Running Braves must have been some studs."

"I don't believe that stuff."

"I believe anything that works," said Brooks. "Quicker you get into shape, quicker we can bring you back to the city to work out in Donatelli's Gym."

"You're serious."

"You think I'm blowing smoke?"

He wanted to ask Brooks if he had used him to lead him to Stick, if he had expected him to hit Lieutenant Deeks and get into X-Men, but he didn't want to risk an answer that would chill the warmth of the moment. So he said, "Don't know."

"You'll find out." For an instant Brooks'

eyes seemed gentle. "I'm sorry how it's worked out for you so far. A lot of it's my fault." Then the eyes hardened. "Got to go, young gentleman. Listen to Jake."

The drive back to the Reservation was long and hot. There was no air-conditioning in the tow truck. On the highway, with the windows open, it was too noisy to talk except in shouts. They were mostly silent until they pulled off at Sparta and headed toward the Res along back roads that became green tunnels boring through forest.

"Tonight," said Jake, "I want you to dream of hawks."

Sonny tried not to laugh. "How come?"

"Give you vision. My grandfather was the last Running Brave. White man knew what powerful medicine it was, what it gave the Moscondaga. White man scared of it."

"Why?"

"People need someone they can look up to. Just being there, the Running Braves gave people hope, strength. Gave 'em the message, You don't have to feel bad about yourself, don't have to drink yourself to death, don't have to do

91

everything the white man says. That's why the white man broke up the Running Braves."

"How?"

"Government men came, said the Running Braves was a secret society, against the law. Threatened the chiefs. Lose government money. Go to jail. And the chiefs got scared and banned the Braves."

He had never heard such a hard, bitter tone in Jake's voice.

"What happened to your grandfather?"

"Your great-great-grandfather. Got killed by a hit-and-run driver. On the Res one morning while he was running. He never stopped running. Wanted to be ready when the Nation needed him again." Jake began to chuckle. "Government men figured the Running Braves died with my grandfather. They didn't know he told me all the secrets. And I been telling you."

11

AN EARTHQUAKE WOKE him, a pounding that rattled his teeth, a booming "Up, get up, let's go." Sonny didn't know where he was—solitary, the hospital, a dream?—until the dogs began howling at the noise.

"LET'S GO!"

He sat up too fast, which made him dizzy, and he jumped out of bed, which sent pain scraping down his scars. Stumbling to the window, he jammed a big toe against the wall. His brain was fogged and his eyes were blurred by sleepers.

Jake was dancing in the moonlight.

The old man wore only a loincloth. He waved a bunch of pine twigs in one hand. When he saw Sonny, he hollered, "Kick a stick." He hopped lightly from bare foot to bare foot.

"You drunk?"

Jake tossed up a stick, caught it neatly on the instep of his left foot and kicked it to his right foot. As he hopped, he passed the stick from foot to foot. "A drunk do this? Come out."

Sonny climbed through the window. "What are you doing?"

"Balance. Footwork. Concentration." He didn't miss a step. "First things a Running Brave learns."

"There are no more Running Braves."

"That's what they think." He flipped a twig at Sonny. "Here." It bounced off Sonny's left foot into the darkness. "'S okay. Got plenty."

Sonny managed to kick the next twig into the air, but he missed it coming down. He kept the third one going for two passes before he stepped on a stone and lost his rhythm.

"This is dumb."

"Only if you can't do it." Jake kicked the twig to eye level and plucked it out of the air with his thumb and forefinger. "Take a mouthful." He pointed the twig at a thermos on the ground. "Don't swallow."

"What is it?"

"Tea. Keep it in your mouth while you kick the stick."

"Why?"

"Learn to breathe through your nose. No

more questions."

Sonny unscrewed the thermos top. A whiff of bitter herbs raked the hairs of his nostrils. "Smells bad."

"Tastes bad, too. Can you hold it for three minutes? One round?"

"Sure." He took a slug. It burned his tongue.

"Here." The stick bounced away off his left foot. He got the rhythm on the next stick, nice and easy, a dance, two, three, I can do this, four, he forgot to breathe through his nose, five, he swallowed, six.

The herb tea burned a furrow down his throat and sizzled in his stomach like molten lava.

It erupted.

Sonny folded forward, an uppercut to the gut, coughing and choking. Last night's dinner bubbled up into his mouth and spilled out in a silvery pool between his feet. When he caught his breath and straightened up, Jake was juggling two sticks with his feet. He wasn't even breathing hard.

"Good exercise." He kicked both sticks overhead and caught them behind his back, one-handed.

Sonny held the second mouthful for more than a minute, kicking away six sticks before he got the timing again, eight passes before he lost the rhythm of breathing through his nose. This time he was braced for the fiery splashdown and the volcanic return, but the aftermath was worse. He retched on an empty stomach, spitting bile. He felt as though the dry heaves would split his scars open.

"You gettin' it," Jake said. "Easier tomorrow."

The night wind prickled the sweat on Sonny's bare skin, a sudden reminder he was wearing only the underwear briefs he had slept in. He must look as ridiculous as Jake did in his old-time leather diaper.

"Try somethin' else now." Jake held his palms together, chest high, as if he were praying. "Arms out straight in front of you."

An old kids' game. Sonny stretched his arms out, his hands on either side of Jake's hands. Off to his left, first light edged the hills of Moscondaga with a pink icing. Dawn soon. Finish this stuff before people start waking up.

"Clap your hands and squash old Jake's paws."

Sonny thought of Brooks making him throw left hooks in the interrogation room. They're always trying to show you up, humiliate you, prove older is better by putting you down. We'll see about that. He felt a familiar feeling coming up his legs into his sore stomach.

He started to dig his bare feet into the sandy soil for better leverage, but Jake was circling to his right with little shuffling sidesteps. The glass eyes of the auto junkyard winked back at the rising light.

Clap.

His palms stung. Jake had dropped his hands at the last instant.

"Stand still." Sonny dug in. *Gonna squash your old paws.*

Clap.

Another clean miss.

"Ain't just reflexes, 'cause yours are faster."

Clap.

Thumbs collided, sending pain up his wrists.

"Training. Look for the muscle twitch, eye shift, quick breath, some signal I'm gonna move my hands."

Clap.

His hands felt hot.

"Running Braves listen with their eyes, study people." The light behind Jake rose into the sky. Sonny couldn't see the old man's eyes.

Clap.

His arms and shoulders ached.

"Keep 'em up," said Jake. He was in silhouette. "Watch for signals."

It was dawn, the sky was a light blue and he couldn't see Jake's eyes. He could barely see his hands.

Clap . . . clap . . . clap . . .

His upper body was on fire, the scars had all torn open, his guts were slithering out into the dust and the rising sun blinded him.

The monster said, Throw the hook, he's right in front of you now, he deserves it. He swallowed the monster down and tasted his own vomit. He tricked you, he didn't play fair, he didn't tell you the key to the game was position. He maneuvered you into the sun.

"Stop," said Jake. "Learn anything?"

"You always got to know where you are."

The old man grunted. "Maybe you ain't as dumb as you look. One more little game."

He motioned Sonny to sit down on the

ground, cross his legs. "Remember the animal alphabet?"

"Heard it enough as a kid."

"Listen real close. When I'm done, I'm gonna ask you one question. Ready?"

"Go." He felt wide awake, his mind and body emptied and open.

"The Creator gave the ant strength beyond its size, taught the beaver to build, the coyote to trick. The deer got speed and the elephant got a good memory. You remember all that, Sonny?"

"Keep going." He wasn't going to let Jake distract him. He made a mental picture of each animal's gift. He'd be ready when Jake asked his question.

"Fox got slyness, goat don't get discouraged, the hawk has vision, the iguana change color, the jackrabbit's quick, the kangaroo got a baby pocket, the loon got a special voice, am I going too fast for you?"

"No problem."

"Monkey smart, nightingale sings, owl is wise, possum can play dead, queen bee knows how to boss, the rattlesnake's got poison, the snipe can go real deep with its bill, turtle's steady, vulture eat anything, wolf's got a pack, the X-ray eel can zap you good, yak's strong and zebra's got stripes." Jake grinned triumphantly. "Ain't done that in a while. So?"

"So what's the question?"

"Just asked it. What didn't you hear?" Jake chuckled and rocked on his bony haunches. "Something missing. What?"

Another trick. Sonny felt suddenly small and stupid. "I don't know."

"The letter u. No creature for u." Jake slapped his knee. "People can only think of one thing at a time. You can confuse 'em, set 'em off in another direction. But a Running Brave got to be thinking everything all the time."

"I had enough." Sonny stood up. What am I doing here in my underpants in the middle of this sad-ass slum with an old crazy? "This isn't going to work."

"Running Braves concentrate, listen, think."

"You're just getting off on me, Jake. Sticks and clapping and kids' games. You've seen too many movies. Think this is some kind of Redskin Karate Kid?"

"Japs smart, too," said Jake. "Good fighters. Had to kill a few in the Big War. That's why I couldn't be a chief. Moscondaga chiefs can't have human blood on their hands."

"You couldn't be a chief because you live in the past, you believe in fairy tales."

Jake stood up. "What's your excuse?"

"Huh?"

"For feeling sorry for yourself, for letting life happen to you 'stead of grabbing at it. You got a chance here, get in shape, learn to box, maybe be a fighter. Brooks thinks you can really do it. I'm not so sure. You got the worst of both sides."

"What does that mean?"

"The white side thinks you're too good to work hard, and the Indian side thinks you're not good enough to make it."

Around them the Reservation stirred, cars growled to life, doors slammed, stoves clattered. Sonny felt naked.

"Now you got to get the best of both sides." Jake slapped his arm. "Get some clothes on. Make you breakfast."

Jake was waiting for him on the back porch with pitchers of water and orange juice and a large bowl of oatmeal. A golden coin of honey stared up from the center of the cereal. "Soothe your stomach. Start drinking eight glasses of water every day, two glasses of juice."

Jake watched him eat. "Walk around the house to digest, then go back to sleep. When you wake up, we'll go for a little run."

He followed Jake's pointing finger past the auto junkyard to the hills of Moscondaga, green in the morning sun, striped with twisting brown trails. "Each day we run a little more, carry more weight. One day we'll run up to Stonebird. Leave you there."

The oatmeal soothed his stomach. Jake mixed water and juice in a glass. It went down easy. He felt better.

"After the solo, you be ready."

"For Donatelli's Gym?"

"To follow the Hawk," said Jake.

12

PAIN CHEWED AT every angle and crevice of his body. His toes hurt, his hips hurt, his eyelids. A hammer pounded his swollen red scars. But Jake pushed him through it. "'S okay, just pain," he'd say, and they'd jog on along the trail, Jake humming, Sonny gasping. His hands ached from squeezing chunks of tire rubber from the junkyard to build up his wrists and forearms. His insteps were raw from the dawns' bare-foot stick dances.

The first week was a blur. Jake shook him awake at first light and dragged him outside to stretch and bend and twist until skin and muscle and tendon burned. Then they would kick the sticks from foot to foot and back and forth between them in ever more complicated patterns. After breakfast and a long walk, there would be word games and string games, then a run. The rising sun softened the edges of his mind, like a flame on wax. He thought only of his training now, each day denser, more difficult, more painful. He chopped wood to build up his shoulders and back. He leaped across the creek, from slippery stone to slippery stone, to improve his balance. He sensed they were being watched by others on the Res, he thought of the wolves and mountain lions of Whitmore. Jake didn't seem to care. Once, when they both noticed the sudden glint of sunlight on the distant lenses of binoculars, Jake just chuckled and said, "Chiefs'll send someone over soon, check us out."

He helped Jake in the junkyard. They prospected through the acres of crumpled cars for an odd part someone had called for, a dashboard gauge from a rare imported car, an antique hood ornament, the motor from a discontinued model. He enjoyed working with Jake, feeling useful. They didn't talk much, pulling away rotting seat cushions, grunting as small animals leaped out to set the dogs barking ferociously in pursuit, straining together to lift out an engine.

A good find meant they'd drive into Sparta to deliver the part, then use some of the cash for a load of meat and vegetables and fruit, and on the way back a video cassette, sometimes the karate movies Jake liked, often a boxing tape. They would watch until one of them began to yawn.

At night Jake sat on the edge of Sonny's bed, pressing his thumbs into the tender muscles of Sonny's legs and back, kneading out the pain, crooning stories.

"One time, on a mission for the Nation, my grandfather got bit on the leg by a rattler. Knew if he kept moving, poison go to his heart. So he shut himself down. Put himself into the 'little death.' Closed down his veins and arteries, slowed his breathing to just enough to keep his brain alive. Saw the suns rise and fall but he couldn't count 'em. Lay there all alone 'cept for his spirit. The Hawk kept watch over him. Finally, his brother Running Braves found him, sucked out the poison and carried him to a medicine man."

"Fairy tale," mumbled Sonny, sliding into sleep under Jake's massaging fingers.

And then it was time to get up again, to kick the stick and run, to chop wood, to leap from slippery stone to slippery stone along the creek.

One of the younger subchiefs finally

strolled into the yard, pretending to look for an engine part.

"Seen you runnin'."

"Yeah."

"Got a fight?"

"Not right away."

"Watch yourself now."

"What's that mean?" snapped Jake.

"Heard about Hillcrest."

"Robbed his fight," said Jake.

"Don't need no more enemies," said the subchief.

"Not with you for a friend," said Jake.

The dogs crowded around, growling at the harshness in their voices. The subchief shrugged and walked away.

Jake raised his voice so the subchief could hear him. "His grandfather sat on the Council when they banned the Braves."

Sonny was surprised by the fury in Jake's voice. "That was a long time ago."

"Some things don't change," said Jake. "That's why this ain't Onondaga or Mohawk, where they got strong chiefs."

Sonny laughed. "That's why you live by yourself, nobody comes to visit."

Jake grinned. "Let 'em think I'm just a crazy old Redskin hearing footprints. Be real surprised one day."

That night they watched a video cassette of Muhammad Ali's greatest fights. Sonny was surprised at the chances Ali took in the ring, leaning back from punches instead of letting them slip past him.

"Hard to learn boxing from him," said Jake. "He had his own special way. But you can learn from him outside the ring. He was of his people. White man gave him a hard time, tried to make him give up his religion, join the Army, say things he didn't believe. Wouldn't let him fight for a long time. But he stood up for what he thought was right."

Later, massaging Sonny's legs in bed, Jake said, "Some black people gave Ali a hard time, too. Everybody's got an idea what you should be, especially if you get big. Maybe you find out, Sonny." He slapped his thigh. "Now sleep."

And then one morning he sat up in bed before Jake arrived. It was still dark, that cool, silent moment before dawn in the hour of the wolf.

Something was different. He waited until

his eyes cleared of sleep and adjusted to the moonlight streaming through the window before his eyes cut a path around the room and out into the yard. Nothing. He listened until the night sounds separated and became distinct, the chatter of the bird talk and the rhythm of insects and the rustle of grass and tree branch. Familiar. He felt the breeze lift the hairs on his arms and he tasted its moisture. He sniffed the scents of different firewoods. Nothing new there.

No pain.

There was no pain this morning. That was the difference. He lay back and closed his eyes and listened to his body from his toes to the roots of his hair. He felt strong.

I can do this thing. Get in shape. Won't be long now before I'm ready for Stonebird. Ready to climb to the top of the highest mountain of Moscondaga with a hundred pounds of stones on my back, and stay there alone with the snakes and the wolves and the mountain lions, and the scariest creatures of all, the dark shapes of the future that lurk in the corners of my mind. I will think about my life, and I will come down the mountain, ready to go back to the city, to Donatelli's Gym. To be a fighter.

Brooks will be there.

And Doll.

"How you feel?" asked Jake, startling him. He hadn't heard him come into the room.

"Good."

Jake cackled. "Take care of that real quick."

That morning he began running with a stone in each hand. A new circuit of pain began across the tops of his shoulders. But the pain was different now, it was welcome. Bring it, I can handle it. Soon it would be gone, too, and the muscles would be stronger.

As he felt better, the monster stirred, an echo, a shadow, a faraway whisper. He pushed it away. But it was there and it made him uneasy. Would he become strong enough to keep the monster in its place?

They were hiking along a fire trail one afternoon, Sonny huffing under fifty pounds of stones in a pack on his back, Jake widening the trail with a rusted, chipped machete he whipped back and forth as if it were an extension of his bony arm, when the old man suddenly stopped and pointed the chipped blade toward the concrete high rises of Sparta.

"Far's your eye, once was Moscondaga," said Jake. "Now look."

Sonny followed the machete tip down the mountain. The Reservation looked so small from here, a pathetic huddle of shabby buildings in a clearing—the elders' Long House, the Christian church, community center, general store. Most of the houses were cabins or mobile homes scattered around the graveyard and the quarry lake. Jake's house was a yellow box in a field of glinting metal and glass. The deep, dark woods he had loved were only a sparse cluster of balding trees.

"All's left," said Jake. "Figure what happened?"

"White man stole it." Sonny was startled at the anger in his voice. The Indian side.

"Some chiefs sold us out, too. White man couldn't done it by himself. Not if we were strong together."

"You think the Braves would've made a difference?"

Jake turned. "The Braves come out of the People."

"What do you mean?"

"If the People want to be strong, there'll be

Braves to help them be what they want." He raised his right hand. "Look."

Very slowly, he pushed his thumb between his third and fourth fingers and curled his hand into a fist. "The Brave is of the People. Part of the People. He gets his strength from the People, he gives strength to the People. This is the sign of the Running Braves. It's a secret."

"So why are you showing me . . ." Sonny stopped. He felt suddenly chilled under the hot afternoon sun.

"There's gonna be big troubles here some-day," said Jake. His eyes were bright. "White man's gonna figure out he can use this raggedy place. For gambling maybe, or to dump garbage. Laws are different on the Res. Gonna wave big money around. Moscondagas gonna be set against each other. Chiefs ain't strong enough to hold the Nation together. The People gonna need a Brave."

"Jake, don't start—"

But the old man was already striding back down the fire trail, whipping the machete, humming tunelessly. Sonny hitched the pack of stones high on his back and hurried after him.

They were almost back at the junkyard before Sonny caught up.

There was a gray stretch limo outside Jake's house. As they approached, a chauffeur jumped out to open a back door for Sonny's mother.

13

H E WAS SURPRISED, as usual, by the loveliness of her face, round and dark and soft, framed by the thick black braids that fell over her bare shoulders. Her blouse was embroidered with an ancient Onondaga design, but it was cut too low in front for any Indian woman to wear in a ceremony. Her brown leather pants were tight on her slim hips.

He was embarrassed when she hugged him and kissed him on the lips. She squeezed his biceps and said, "Wow," then pushed him out to arm's length.

"You look . . . harder." Her brow furrowed, but then she smiled and hugged him again. "Oh, Sonny, I've got such wonderful news. I've found our special place. In Phoenix. You'll have your own room, we can blow this dump today."

"Dump, Answedaywe?" There was sarcasm in the way Jake said her Moscondaga name.

"Oh, Uncle Jake." She threw her arms

around his neck. "You know what I mean."

"What do you mean?" asked Jake.

A tall white man, elegantly wrapped in a pale-gray suit that matched the limo, put a large hand on her bare shoulder. She patted it.

"This is my . . . friend. Roger."

"How are ya?" He waved at Jake, who had sidled out of handshake range. Roger gave Sonny's hand a brisk pump. "Sonny, you always got a place at Sweet Bear's Kiva."

"Sweet Bear's what?" asked Jake.

"That's what we're calling the boutiques," said Sonny's mother quickly. "Roger operates luxury hotels in Chicago, Minneapolis and Phoenix. We're going to open authentic Indian shops in the lobbies."

"Authentic." Jake rolled his eyes. "Kiva is not in our language."

"For your foreign tourist," said Roger, "Indian is Indian. Just so long as they get native goods. They don't want Hong Kong wampum, if you get my drift." He had a booming voice that reminded Sonny of TV car salesmen.

"Come on in," said Jake. "Hot out here."

Roger glanced at a heavy gold wristwatch. "Wheels up in an hour."

"Roger's corporate jet," said Sonny's

mother proudly. "We've got a marketing meeting in Chicago tonight."

"Come for some native goods?" asked Jake.

"I've come for Sonny."

"How long this time?" The old man's voice was steelier than Sonny had ever heard it.

"For good," she said.

"Heard that before," said Jake.

"Sonny, go pack," said Roger. "Take what you need for a week. Jake can ship the rest."

She smiled at Sonny. "You'll love Phoenix."

"I want to stay here."

"We'll be together. You can work in the shops."

"I want to stay with Jake."

"There's nothing for you here."

Sonny took a deep breath. "I'm in training to be a fighter."

"Jake!" The softness was gone from her face and voice. Her bird eyes pecked at the old man. "Sonny's got a chance to be somebody now. I'm not going to let you spoil it."

"Chop chop," said Roger, tapping his watch. "Gotta go."

"You go," said Sonny. His hands curled into fists.

Roger backed toward the limo. "Work it

out, Sweet." He climbed back inside and slammed the door, disappearing behind the dark tinted window.

"Let him stay," said Jake. "He's doing real good."

"Don't get in my way, Jake. I'm not leaving without him. And if that means the sheriff, I'll call him."

Sonny looked at Jake, who nodded. "She can do it, boy. Come on, I'll help you pack." He grabbed Sonny's elbow and roughly steered him into the house. "No trouble. Get him on his way. Sweet."

"Make it snappy, Jake. No tricks."

Inside, Jake said, "Time to go to Donatelli's Gym."

"What about Stonebird?"

"Stonebird ain't the only mountain."

Sonny's mouth went dry. "Am I ready?"

"Find out." Jake rummaged in a drawer. "Here." He pressed money into Sonny's hand. "Keys in the truck. Stay on back roads to Syracuse, then use the Thruway. Call me from New York."

"I don't know the way to Donatelli's Gym."

"Hundred-twenty-fifth Street and Seventh

116

Avenue. Harlem." Jake raised his right hand, thumb tucked between the third and fourth fingers. "Don't forget, you of the People."

"I'm not a Running Brave, Jake."

"Not yet."

14

IT WAS NEARLY midnight before he found the Harlem street. The Korean grocery on the corner was bright with fresh fruits and vegetables and bustling with customers. The second-floor law offices were dark. A single light on the third floor glowed behind the letters on the dusty window—DONATELLI'S GYM. Sonny double-parked the tow truck.

A Korean man shelling peas on the sidewalk shouted, "No park," but Sonny strode past him, through the wooden door and onto the dark steps.

He knew he should take a deep breath, wait for his eyes to adjust to the darkness, move cautiously up the narrow, twisting stairs, but all he had thought about on the long drive from the Res was getting to the top of the stairs, into the gym and on with his journey.

He took the steps two at a time, feeling them sag under his pounding weight. Wood screeched, his boots slipped on the worn-smooth steps, he fell to one knee, could be a guard dog up there, but he couldn't slow himself down, a guy with a bat up there, a gun, too late to stop he scraped his shoulder against the wall, light leaked through the crack under the door marked GYM, he took a breath and threw open the door and plunged into the murky room.

"What took you so long, young gentleman?"

Brooks was sitting on a wooden folding chair under the only light in the room, a naked bulb hanging on a cord from the ceiling. He was dressed for a workout, high-topped black boxing shoes, trunks. His tee-shirt was dark with sweat. Punching-bag mitts were on the floor beside him.

"Jake called me." Brooks took a long pull on a bottle of water. He pointed to a chair facing him and waited for Sonny to sit.

"Life is funny. I came up those stairs the same way you did, alone, at night, running scared. Twenty years ago. Mr. Donatelli sat in this chair and looked right inside me and figured I'd never be much of a boxer, but if he gave me a chance to train here, I might be able to beat the streets, be a contender."

The softness of his voice drew Sonny forward, straining to hear. Sonny felt his heart beating.

"You know what a contender is?" Brooks didn't wait for an answer. "A guy coming up, willing to bust his tail and take his lumps to find out just how far he can go. Mr. Donatelli said it's the climbing that makes the man, that getting to the top is an extra reward. You believe that?"

Sonny shrugged.

"You got to make a commitment to yourself before you make one to anything else. You got to decide to have pride, to act smart, to take control of your life. Control. You know what I mean?"

Sonny nodded.

"That thing inside you. What Jake calls the spirit. The Hawk. Mr. Donatelli believed there was a fire inside. He used to say a fire can keep you warm and cook your food, or it can burn you to death. Fire's not good or bad, it's just something you've got to control. Fear is that fire. Most people either let fear control them or spend all their energy keeping that fear bottled up. The great champions use that fear—they turn it into fury when they need it. You learn to do that, you can beat anything, anywhere."

Brooks stood up and pulled a dangling string. Sonny blinked at the sudden dazzling light of a dozen or more naked bulbs. Brooks leaned against the ring ropes.

"From now on, this is your life. Run every morning, train every afternoon, go to fights, watch fight movies, read about fights. And Rocky. You got to put in your rounds with Rocky."

Brooks pointed across the room at a life-sized stuffed dummy hanging from the ceiling by a thick chain. The dummy's canvas skin was divided into squares from forehead to waist, each with a number. "Mr. Donatelli invented the system, after my time, and Henry perfected it when he took over the gym. Sharpens your reflexes, gets you thinking about combinations."

"I can do it."

"Anybody can do it. Rocky doesn't have arms to hit you back. And training's the easy part. There are rules here. Henry has his rules and I have mine. You're going to sleep here, and you're gonna keep this place clean. That's how you pay for your training. Every night, you sweep the gym and mop it and scrub the blood off the canvas, and wash the bathrooms and showers and whatever else Henry tells you. Got that?"

Sonny nodded. He felt excited. This was for real.

"The only time you leave this place alone is to run in the morning. Don't want you wandering around the neighborhood. Don't want you spotted by X-Men. And I'm only going to say this once." Brooks' voice dropped. "Stick and Doll are out of your life. If you go down to The Deuce, don't come back. Got that?"

He nodded.

"You got talent. You could go all the way. But before you beat anybody else, you got to beat yourself. And this is sink-or-swim territory. Henry'll tell you right off it's no therapy group. I'll help you all I can, but it's like a fight— you got to do this by yourself."

There was a hammering knock on the door.

Sonny froze. His mom must have called the sheriff in Sparta, who called New York. It was over before it had begun.

The Korean man stuck his head in. "Truck block way."

"Be right down, Kim," said Brooks. "Want you to meet Sonny. He's going to take care of this place."

"Hard job," said Kim.

"Great job," said Brooks. "Could be worth millions."

15

"**T**HIS IS NO THERAPY group," said Henry Johnson, "no training program for minorities, no rehab-detox-support center. This is a *pro*-fessional boxing gymnasium. You got it?"

Sonny nodded.

Johnson pulled at his little beard and frowned as if he wasn't so sure Sonny got it. "I seen this before. Kid watches a Rocky movie and comes in here looking to be champ. Hate those Rocky movies. That's why I call him Rocky." He tapped the life-sized dummy swinging from the ceiling. "I'm going to show you this just once."

He squared off in front of Rocky. Johnson was tall and thin. He walked with a slight limp. He wore a white shirt and a tie. "Your partner calls the punches. Like so. Jab . . . one."

He didn't look like a fighter, but the punch Johnson threw at Rocky's head was brisk and precise. It landed on the point of Rocky's canvas chin, in the square marked 1.

"In the beginning you just practice your punches, how you throw them, where they land. Right . . . eight."

A straight right landed on the numbered square on Rocky's left eye.

"After a while you'll go for combinations. Jab . . . five. Right . . . six. Hook . . . seven. Right . . . nineteen." He grunted as his right uppercut thumped into Rocky's belly. "You got it?"

"Yeah," said Sonny.

"Your partner'll be Martin Witherspoon. He comes by every day after school. You can take two hours off to train. That's your time." Johnson surveyed the empty gym, dusty in the early-morning sunlight. "Rest of the time is mine. Hot plate in my office, cook your meals there, make sure you pull the plug when you're done. Wash your dishes. Anything you leave in the fridge, you mark your name on it. Use the TV if you like. No visitors overnight, no smoking, no drugs. Any questions?"

"No."

"Start mopping."

"Jab . . . five . . . five."

Martin Witherspoon was a big fat black kid with round glasses that made him look like an owl. His voice was low and bored. For three minutes he droned out the commands. When the bell rang to end the round, he turned away and picked his nose or pulled at the wedgie in the seat of his tight black pants. He looked as though he wanted to be somewhere else. Anywhere else.

"Right . . . sixteen."

Every other training partner in the gym snapped out the punches like bingo numbers, urgent and sharp. Why had Johnson stuck him with Martin? Didn't care? Just looking for a free janitor? Sonny began to imagine Martin's face divided into numbered squares.

"Right . . . two. Jab . . . seven."

Martin's monotone hung heavy on Sonny's arm, slowed his reflexes, dulled his brain. He was pushing at Rocky instead of hitting him. He was tired anyway. At four o'clock in the afternoon he needed a cheerleader, not a sleep talker. By four he had already put in a full day.

An old-fashioned alarm clock jangled him awake at five o'clock on mornings he hadn't already been jerked out of sleep by screams or gunshots or police sirens. From the cot he could watch a grotesque parade of shapes across the ceiling, shadows thrown up by passing cars and trucks.

They reminded him of his junkyard drawings. He thought about the sketchbook in the deerskin pack. The Deuce. Doll. Would he ever see her again? Brooks said, If you go down to The Deuce, don't come back. But someday, when I'm somebody, with some money, a pro boxer, I'll go find her, take her off The Deuce.

He never got too far with that scenario. If it came to him at night, he would usually fall asleep in the middle of it. There was never any time to dream in daylight. Up at dawn, fold the cot, roll it into the utility closet where the mops and pails waited for him to scrub and wipe the bathroom, to sweep and swab the gym floor, the locker room, the shower room, and Johnson's private office.

While the floors dried, he stretched and bent and twisted, then kicked a pencil from foot to foot until he did it without a miss for three minutes. Then out to run. It was the best part of the day.

The fifteen blocks to Central Park was his warm-up, an easy three quarters of a mile over concrete, broken glass, crack vials, pools of wine and vomit, banana peels, chicken bones, oil smears. He hurdled the cardboard homes and the ragged lumps wheezing in sleep. When he hit the park, he shifted his body into overdrive.

The sounds of the city were muffled in the park, birds chirped, squirrels and rats scampered across the soft earth that cushioned his steps. The dark green soothed and strengthened him. He ran hard for an hour in a wide circle that took him downtown toward the luxury apartment buildings with penthouses overlooking the park. He wondered if he would ever make enough money to live in one. He wondered what the house in Phoenix looked like. He was glad Mom had something going for herself now, and he wished he could tell her he was okay, too. But she'd never understand how he could be living in a gym in Harlem thinking he was okay. She'd send the sheriff down if she knew. Even Jake didn't understand. He tried to make it more than it was. On the phone, Jake kept saying it was like Stonebird, only a different kind of solo.

No way. It was just what it was. A chance to be somebody.

The run always ended too soon. He came back out of the park into the morning rush hour, streets jammed with hot metal screeching, honking, farting fumes, sidewalks jammed with men and women hurrying to work, children to school. The traffic slowed him to a walk. Sometimes he thought he got suspicious glances from the beeper dudes, but he just kept moving. He was careful not to eyeball anyone. He didn't notice any tattooed X's.

At the Korean grocery on the corner he bought oranges and muffins. Upstairs he boiled water for coffee on the hot plate. He missed the eggs and cereal and toast that Jake had made for him, but his money was starting to run low. He would be finished eating by the time the early birds came chattering up the steps, a few businessmen and politicians who worked in Harlem and liked to skip rope and hit the bags while they gossiped about real-estate deals and what the mayor was going to do next. They didn't need much attention besides getting towels for the shower. The real fighters didn't start drifting in until the late morning, and they always came with their managers and trainers and sparring partners and pals. One heavyweight, Dave

Reynolds, a loud guy whose handlers all wore black silk jackets with DAVE THE FAVE stitched on the back, brought along his own disc jockey, a guy who did nothing but program the portable compact disc player the fighter trained to. He was into rap. Some of the other fighters didn't like it too much, but the Fave was the number-eight-ranked contender, and he had a big fight in Atlantic City coming up.

The Fave never noticed Sonny. Nobody did, except to call for extra towels or tell him to mop up after a blood spill or send him out for food. That usually meant a free lunch. When one of the pro trainers gave him money for Chinese or sandwiches or fried chicken, he almost always told Sonny to feed himself from the change.

He tried to pick up pointers as the trainers shouted instructions at their fighters. He watched the pros throw their punches, make their moves in the ring, hit the bag, shadow-box. They knew what they were doing. They were serious workers. Some of them were preparing for matches in Atlantic City and at Madison Square Garden.

Most of them were finished with their training by the late afternoon, when the schoolkids and the yuppies and the beginning pro boxers who needed to keep their day jobs arrived. One of Johnson's sons took over Sonny's chores for two hours while Sonny did his sit-ups and push-ups, skipped rope, punched the bags, shadowboxed and pounded Rocky to Martin Witherspoon's monotone. He grew to hate the fat owl, the way he gasped for air after the three-story climb, the way he kept pushing his round glasses up his sweaty nose, the drone of his voice.

"Jab . . . one. Hook . . . two."

His sessions on Rocky grew shorter. He began to lose interest. He even stopped getting angry when a squat heavyweight who arrived at the gym in a postal carrier's uniform tapped him on the shoulder and said, "'Nuff lovin' for Rocky today, my man—let The Punching Postman put some real hurt down."

He began to wish Brooks would come by. At night, waiting for the laundry machines to finish the towels and the jockstraps and the workout clothes, he thought about Doll and The Deuce. Brooks had said, Go down there and don't come back.

Might just do that.

Dinner was some more food picked up at the Koreans', something easy he could cook on the hot plate, or something from the salad bar. Sometimes he fell asleep in front of an old movie on TV. Sometimes he just watched the dark shapes roll across the ceiling until they swallowed him.

16

"**R**IGHT . . . ONE."

He sensed a familiar presence behind him before he heard the voice. "You're thinkin' about sittin' around the fire 'stead of choppin' the wood."

"Who're you?" asked Martin.

"Got to concentrate, Sonny," said Jake. "When a Running Brave chops wood, he thinks about the tree and the axe, not the fire he's gonna make."

"That is so cool," said Martin. "What's a Running Brave?"

Jake ignored him. "You practicing to hit a man, Sonny. So you think flesh. Jaw's hard, sting your hand. Belly soft, slow your punches. Hit the nose right, drive a bone into his brain."

Jake whirled on Martin and fired a bony finger at the owl face. "When you call a number, you gotta think, Why? Number nine, eye, so he can't see what's coming next. Number twenty-five, arm, deaden his muscle so

133

he can't hit you so hard." He stalked off toward Johnson's office.

"Who was that?" Martin's eyes seemed even rounder than his glasses.

"My great-uncle."

"He some kind of shaman?"

"What?"

"You know, like an elder . . ."

"He's old, for sure." Sonny cocked his fists at Rocky. "Let's go!"

"Jab . . . one . . . one. Right . . . three. Jab . . . one. . . . Where's he live?"

"Don't stop."

"Hook . . . five. Jab . . . one . . . one. Right . . . six."

They worked on Rocky for five more rounds, a hot blur, Martin's voice bingo urgent, Sonny lost in the intensity of his concentration as his pounding fists moved over the dummy's body.

"Time!" Johnson was staring at him. "You been flat-foot when you jab. Up on the balls of your feet. More forward. See?" He demonstrated and walked away. It was the first time Johnson had given him any instruction since he had started.

Martin wiped his glasses. "Man, that was awesome. You tapped into a spiritual well-spring."

"You woke up." Sonny strode to the mirrors, Martin at his heels.

"Is he like a wise man, your uncle?"

"Runs a junkyard."

"This is like a movie. You see *American Ninja*? *Karate Kid*?"

Sonny began to shadowbox at his reflection in the mirror.

"He live in the city?"

"On the Reservation. He came to get his truck."

"Reservation? What kind of Native American are you?"

"Half Moscondaga, half white."

"That is so cool. What does Sonny Bear mean?"

"It's my name."

"Yeah, but does it have some tribal significance, like when a bear came to the wigwam . . ."

"No. My dad's name was B-a-y-e-r, people pronounced it bear, so that's the way my mom started spelling it when we went to the pow-wows."

"Powwows! What were they like, what did you . . ."

"You're blocking the mirror." He almost felt sorry for pushing Martin out of his way. He had never seen him excited before, shifting from foot to foot as the words tumbled out of his mouth.

"I thought you were just some wiseguy with a ponytail. Listen, maybe we could . . . Uh-oh."

The change in his voice made Sonny turn. A tall, gray-haired man in a pin-striped suit stood at the door talking to Johnson. When he spotted Martin, he waved him over with a commanding swing of his arm.

"Gotta go. My dad. See you tomorrow around noon?"

"We don't start till . . ."

"I'll help you clean up so we can plan our attack on Rocky." He made it sound like a war movie. "See ya." Martin waddled away.

Jake helped Sonny restack the chairs and straighten up after the gym cleared out. They ate dinner at a Chinese restaurant across the street.

"Always train with that boy?"

"He really got into it after you laid that Braves stuff on us."

"Think they love Indians, new-age yappies."

"Yuppies."

"'S okay. He can help you if you let him."

"How?"

"Every Running Brave had a young warrior-in-training he . . ."

"C'mon, Jake, none of that."

Jake said, "Your mom been calling."

"Yeah?" He felt glad and scared.

"She don't like it, you down here by yourself."

"What's she gonna do?"

"Don't know. Limo fella keeps her busy with"—he spat out the words—"Sweet Bear's Kiva. She wants you out there with her."

"Selling jewelry?"

"Live good. Make some money. Finish school. Not bad."

"Sounds like you think I should go."

Jake shook his head. "I think you got to make the choice."

"I'm not going."

"See what happens. She could try to make you." Jake poured tea. "Know a girl Heather?"

"Heather?"

"Called twice. Said she owes you a slice."

"Heather." His stomach flipped and his face felt hot. Doll wants to see me. "Some girl from Sparta, from high school."

"Sounded long distance." Jake raised his eyebrows. "Maybe somebody you met down here?"

"How would she know to call you?" That night at Stick's. He had run at the mouth. Had he mentioned Jake? "There was a Heather in my homeroom."

Jake stood up. "Gotta feed the dogs." He pulled money out of his jeans, left some on the table to pay the bill and stuffed the rest into Sonny's pocket. "Eat right. Chicken, fish, greens, hot cereal."

They walked to the corner. The tow truck was parked in front of the Korean grocery. Sonny realized he didn't want Jake to leave. "Martin thought you were a wise man."

He expected Jake to grunt, but he smiled. "Let that boy help you. You getting strong now. One time I worried, all alone with your mom, wearing that jewelry, hiding out in the cars to make your little pictures . . ."

"You knew?"

"Been watching you close, Sonny. You got

138

the blood. Started you boxing to get that Hawk out. Now I know you gonna be fine. Gotta go now."

Sonny tried to think of something else to say, to keep him talking on the corner, but he couldn't, and after a while he put out his hand to shake. Jake hugged him. It was the first time Sonny remembered being hugged by Jake since he was little. He watched Jake climb into the truck and drive away. Sonny's eyes were wet.

"Grampada?" Kim was staring up at him.

He sounded so eager that Sonny nodded. "Yeah, my grandpa."

Kim motioned him into the store and held his sleeve while he punched open the cash register and pulled out a photograph of a skinny old man in a black suit. "Kim grampada." He resembled Jake.

"Could be brothers," said Sonny.

Kim laughed and bobbed his head and shook Sonny's hand. "Wait." He plucked a banana and an orange out of their bins. "Here." When Sonny tried to pay him, he pushed the money away.

The phone was ringing when Sonny got upstairs. He hoped it was Doll.

"How you doin', young gentleman?"

"Fine."

"Don't sound positive."

"Jake just left."

Brooks' voice softened. "Miss him already."

"Sort of."

"I'll try to get up soon. Take you to a great soul-food place. I'm really jammed right now—we're running a 24-7-365 surveillance with the feds, wiretap, the works. Major case. Could go down anytime." He sounded tired.

Sonny thought of Stick and Doll. "In the Port?"

Brooks' voice changed gears. "Heard you made war on old Rocky today."

"You got a wiretap here, too?"

Brooks chuckled. "Spoon told me. Martin's dad? Used to be a helluva light heavyweight till he got hurt. Mr. Donatelli made him quit, go to college. He's a school principal now. He and his wife Betty used to . . . Hang on. What's that?" He was yelling to someone else. "Right there. Got to go, young gentleman, talk to you soon." He hung up.

Sonny felt lonely in the spooky silence of the dark gym. He welcomed the grotesque shapes rolling across the ceiling. Old friends. How had Doll gotten Jake's number? He was sure he had never mentioned Jake. The only place the number was written down was on his ID card in the wallet he had lost during the drug bust in the Port.

It took him a long time to fall asleep. She had his wallet. Had she just gotten it? Maybe she was calling to tell him she had just bought it off somebody in the street and wanted to get it back to him. Or maybe she'd had it all the time. Got to find out. And the deerskin pack with his sketchbook. Even worse than losing the wallet was Doll and Stick looking at his pictures.

"Jab . . . seven . . . seven. Right . . . six. Hook . . ."

The notebook in Martin's hand was drenched with sweat and his glasses were sliding down his nose, but his voice was a whiplash.

"Jab . . . three . . . three . . . two. Right . . . sixteen."

The bell rang and they both sucked air. The dummy was pocked with depressions the size of Sonny's gloved fist.

"My dad . . . helped me . . ." gasped Martin, "work out . . . combinations."

A few fighters drifted over to watch Sonny hammer Rocky. Johnson joined them. "Not bad, Sonny."

"Excellent," said Martin.

The Punching Postman snorted. "Rocky can't hit you back."

"True enough," said Johnson. "As Mr. Donatelli used to say, 'The dummy has no arms.'"

"So get us a dummy with arms," said Martin. "Like the mailbag here."

"You fat . . ." The Postman reached for Martin, but Sonny slapped his arms away.

"You want to fight someone, fight me," said Sonny.

"I don't fight amateurs."

Martin slipped behind Sonny. "Postman couldn't lick a stamp."

"You serious, pig meat? I sparred with the Fave last week."

"So you got nothing to worry about." Martin looked at Johnson. "How about it?"

The monster stirred, a good feeling. "I'm ready."

Johnson combed his beard with three fingers. "We don't fight in anger here . . ."

"Right," said the Postman. "This is a *professional* gym."

". . . but it might just be time to see what Sonny's got."

The bells had fallen silent and the bags hung limply. The fighters and trainers gathered expectantly.

"I got three pro fights," howled the Postman. "This kid's nobody."

"Then why you scared?" sneered Martin.

The laughter that swept across the gym darkened the Postman's face. "Now." He stomped up the steps to the ring. "Bud. Hands."

A toothless old man with thick white hair wrapped the Postman's hands in dirty gauze and fresh white tape and stuffed them into pillowy training gloves. When he was finished, he beckoned Sonny up to the ring and repeated the process. He leaned forward as he tied Sonny's laces and whispered, "Postman like to clinch. Belly's weak."

Martin was jittery with excitement. "You can do it, Sonny. Put some hurt on him."

Johnson climbed through the ropes. "It's

over when I say so. Got it?"

Sonny nodded, and the Postman said, "Prepare to be mailed home, sucker. The Postman rings once."

Grinning, the Punching Postman confidently marched to the center of the ring. He fired a right at Sonny's head. Some pro, Sonny thought. The punch was slow and easy to slip.

Martin was yelling, "Jab . . . one . . . one. Right . . . eight—AWWW-RIGHT!"

The Postman took the hook high on his cheek, turned and wobbled into the ropes. He turned back to Sonny, his eyes crossed, his knees knocking. Johnson stepped between them. "It's over."

Too easy, thought Sonny. Just a blowhard, not a pro.

Martin was in the ring, jumping up and down, waving Sonny's arm. "Special Delivery. Express Mail. When Sonny Bear stamps your letter, you are sealed and delivered."

17

"ALFRED BROOKS SAT right where you are now, Sonny," said Martin's father. He was sitting at the head of the dining-room table. "He was one skinny boy."

"We fed him steaks before his fights," said Martin's mother. She fussed at Sonny's plate of spaghetti. "Steaks! That's how much we knew about nutrition in those days, Spoon."

"We were the ones ate the spaghetti." Spoon chuckled and raised his glass to his wife. "Twenty years ago, Betty."

"Time does fly when you're having fun." Denise, Martin's younger sister, rolled her eyes at Sonny. "You must love to have us sit here watch you eat."

He didn't mind at all. He felt their good feelings wash over him as he thought about the fight tonight. First round of an amateur tournament, Brooks had said, you could be up against a hero or a zero. No way to prepare. Stay loose

145

and be ready for anything. Sonny swallowed a mouthful of spaghetti. "No problem."

"No problem," echoed Martin. "I'm planning our moves." He was scratching away in his notebook. "Boxing is merely chess with blood."

"How much blood you spill lately?" sneered Denise.

"Thinking about spilling some of yours, Dumese."

"Children!" said Betty. "Sonny needs a calm atmosphere." She smiled at Sonny. "More salad?"

"No, thanks, this was really good."

"Dad, I got the Tyson-Berbick opening." Martin waved the notebook. "Jab . . . one . . . three. Right . . ."

"You don't want to overplan," said Spoon. "Never lock in so rigidly you lose the option to be flexible. You have to anticipate surprise. Mr. Donatelli said that."

"Mr. Donatelli was one of those wise men," said Martin. "Like Jake."

"He's no wise man," said Sonny.

"Who's Jake?" asked Denise.

"He's like a shaman," said Martin. "An elder of the tribe."

"He runs a junkyard on the Reservation," said Sonny.

"Can't judge a man's wisdom by how he makes his living," said Spoon.

"Enough talk," said Betty. "Let Alfred digest . . ." She laughed. "I mean Sonny."

Denise said, "Mom's in a time warp."

"You're just warped," said Martin. "I'll take Sonny for a walk, then he can lie down."

"I'll come, too," said Denise.

"Skip that," snapped Martin. "We've got . . ."

"I need you to help me, Denise," said Betty.

Out on the street, Martin said, "Denise got the warms for you. You got a girl?"

Sonny thought of Doll. "Sort of." He pushed her out of his mind. Not now. Stay loose. "Always live here?" The neighborhood was quiet and old, crumbly red brick apartment buildings along grimy sidewalks. Most of the people they passed were old whites and young blacks and Latinos.

"My folks been here forever. It's okay. When the geeps come from Jersey to score rocks off the Dominicans, it wakes up. At least one shootout per weekend. You have crack on the Reservation?"

"Not like here, but a kid might bring something back from Sparta. Chiefs better not find out."

"What would they do?"

"Kick butt. Maybe send some warriors down to Sparta to warn the dealers off."

Martin's eyes were wide. "They can do that?"

"Moscondagas are pretty tough, not like the old days, of course. There was this society of warriors called the Running Braves . . ."

He stopped himself. Playing Indian. Listening for footprints. "Some other time."

"Sure, I understand. Mess your mind up before a fight. This must be like a different planet for you."

"What do you mean?"

"You know, whites, blacks, all together, city."

"No. My mom traveled a lot. I don't remember when we lived in New York, but I remember L.A. and Santa Fe and Minneapolis. I liked Santa Cruz a lot, Miami." It was easy talking to Martin. He felt as though he was outside himself, listening.

"Your mom didn't like the Res?"

"No. She used to say, 'The only time I want

to be on the Res is when the world ends, because everything happens on the Res ten years later.'"

"I thought you lived with Jake."

"Some of the time."

"He coming tonight?"

"You never know with Jake."

"What about Brooks?"

"What about him?"

"He's real interested in you."

"How you know that?" Sonny felt his heart speed up.

"Hear him talking to my dad."

"Like what?"

"Like how much talent you got to be a great fighter if you get control over yourself."

He tried to sound casual. "What's he think?"

"Says it's up to you."

They circled the block twice before Martin brought him back upstairs and into his bedroom. The walls were covered with posters for Save the Earth concerts. There was even a Grateful Dead poster. The shelves were crammed with magazines, books and computer disks. There were two computer monitors on a desk in one corner. "One's for homework, one's for writing," said Martin.

"What do you write?"

"Stories. Maybe I'll write a book about you when you're champ."

Sonny pulled off his boots and stretched out on Martin's bed. "You getting this down? The champ's got a hole in his right sock."

"Right now I'm writing up our fight plans. Operation Rocky."

"Don't overplan." Sonny felt his body relax. He felt safe in this house and easy with this fat owl. He closed his eyes and started to drift away. "Remember what your dad said."

"He's always putting me down."

Something in Martin's voice snapped him awake. "How come?"

"He was a big jock, could have been light-heavyweight champ if he didn't get hurt, and he thinks I'm just a blob who reads too much. That's why he made me go to the gym. I hated it till you came around."

Sonny laughed. "You mean till Jake came around."

Martin laughed, too. "What about your dad?"

Sonny pointed to the wall. "Grateful Dead

was his favorite band. He died in Vietnam. That's all I know. Nobody talks about him."

"Sorry."

Sonny closed his eyes again.

At twilight, Betty woke him up and made him drink tea with honey. She gave him a hug at the door, and Denise kissed his cheek. They said they wouldn't be at the fight but they'd be thinking of him. Martin seemed tense. For once he didn't have much to say as Spoon drove them to a large, shabby building across the East River from Manhattan. The marquee advertised an afternoon dog show and an evening of amateur bouts, the first round of the Gotham Gloves.

Johnson was waiting for them. "Sonny's on early. Might as well go inside."

"Alfred here?" asked Spoon.

"Not yet."

The smell of dogs still hung in the arena. A boxing ring had been set up in the center of the main hall, surrounded by folding chairs. Sonny thought it looked like a larger version of the hillbilly smokers. He wondered if they'd try the same thing here, give the fight to the home-town boy.

Let 'em try. He began to feel excitement build from his toes.

The locker room was crowded with a dozen young fighters in their undershorts waiting to be weighed and examined while their trainers and fathers and friends rubbed them and made conversation. The room smelled of liniment and nervous sweat.

"Sonny Bear?" called a man in a red blazer.

"Over here," said Johnson.

"Third bout. Black trunks," said the man, tapping his clipboard. "Let's go."

Sonny weighed in at 185. The doctor examined his mouth and eyes, checked the inside of his arm for needle marks and listened to his heart. "Better calm your boy, Henry," said the doctor to Johnson. "His engine's over the speed limit."

"It's his first fight," said Johnson. "Remember it, Doc. Be historical." He taped Sonny's hands.

The man with the clipboard barked, "Bear-Cooper on deck."

"Hands," snapped Johnson. He pushed the gloves on and laced them. He rubbed Sonny's chest and arms. "You take your time, feel him out the first round, stick and move, don't go for the head too early."

Sonny thought of Jake. Why do they all say the same things? He looked around the locker room. Where was Brooks?

"Bear-Cooper, let's go."

The hot blaze of the arena smacked him in the face. He smelled mustard, beer and the smoke caught in the tunnels of light. People were stamping, clapping, chanting, "Coo-per, Coo-per." Local boy for sure, Sonny thought, have to knock him out just to get a decision.

He barely heard the instructions from the referee as the chants of "Coo-per, Coo-per" swelled to fill the arena, smothering Johnson's "Stick and move, stick and move" and Martin's shrill "Jab . . . one . . . three." The monster roared and surged up into his chest and neck and brain. Sonny thought of wild horses at the ends of leather reins, controlled by the flicks of his wrist.

Cooper was fast and smart, and he knew how to stay away from the left hook. More hero than zero. By the middle of the first round, Sonny felt frustrated, planted like a tree in the middle of the ring while Cooper circled away from Sonny's left so he could never set himself to fire the hook, or even mount a quick barrage of left jabs. The crowd had come for action and they booed.

Sonny stalked back to his corner at the bell. "He won't fight." He dropped onto the stool.

"He's no fool," said Johnson, tilting the water bottle above Sonny's mouth. "Wait your time. And don't listen to the crowd. No one's hitting them." He pushed Sonny out for the second round.

The monster had no patience. He taunted Sonny, This boy's making you look like a wooden Indian—can't you run him into a corner, rattle his bones?

He felt as if he had one foot on the gas and one on the brake, pumping himself into high speed and holding himself back. His mind raced but his body stalled. Stay. Go. Wait. Bang him!

The bell rang. Johnson waved him into the corner and put his mouth to Sonny's ear. "He'll crack. Wait. Pressure's on him not to look scared of you."

The monster said, Jump out and give this Cooper the hook before they steal this fight.

Take control. Go out nice and easy and make him crack.

At the bell, Sonny stood up slowly and strolled to the center of the ring with his hands below his waist. Cooper's eyes narrowed suspiciously. His dark-brown skin was very smooth. Hasn't been hit much, Sonny thought. Doesn't want to get his face scuffed up. Good to know. When Cooper began skipping away, Sonny raised his right arm and beckoned him, smiling, join the party. The crowd applauded.

Cooper darted in and popped two jabs to Sonny's jaw, but they were light and off the mark. He was more interested in getting away without getting hit back than in following the jabs with real punches.

Sonny shook his head until the ponytail was slapping rhythmically against his shoulders. Don't you want to fight?

"Cooper, ya bum," someone shouted.

"Pretty boy."

The crowd laughed. A crumpled paper cup flew into the ring and bounced out. Cooper looked angry.

"Fight, Cooper, you scared a him?"

Cooper cracked. He darted in again, but this time he was moving forward when he threw the jabs and he had his right cocked. He was ready to take a risk to do damage.

Tough luck, Coop.

Sonny let the first jab graze his chin, he slipped the second and when Cooper was close enough he drove a right uppercut into his stomach. It straightened Cooper up.

Sonny glimpsed an open mouth gasping for breath. Hook . . . five closed the mouth. Right . . . six sent him reeling across the ring.

Johnson's voice cut through the roar of the crowd. "Now, Sonny, now."

All yours, monster.

Cooper turned as Sonny hurtled toward him. He threw up his hands in front of his face. Sonny's first hook drove Cooper's own glove into his face and the straight right snapped his head around. The second hook slammed into Cooper's forehead. As he was going down, the referee pushed Sonny away.

Martin howled and tumbled over the ropes to hug him, and Johnson held up his arm as the referee counted Cooper out.

Brooks climbed into the ring, an enormous

grin pushing the tiredness off his face. "Not bad for starters. Sonny."

It was the first time Brooks had called him by name.

18

ROM THE WAIST up Delgado looked like a bodybuilder, smooth muscles popping and rippling under his suntanned skin. His stomach was laid with cobblestones. The crowd whistled when he took off his blue silk robe. Sonny studied Delgado. His legs didn't match the rest of his body. Too thin. Not enough muscle. Not enough roadwork, thought Sonny. I can wear him down.

At the bell, Delgado flexed for the crowd and danced out, smirking. When Sonny backed away, he beckoned and shouted, "C'mon, Sonny boy, my car's double-parked."

The monster chipped in, You don't need to hear that, you can let him land a punch or two, you can take it.

Let Mr. America run his mouth, said Sonny, I'm here to win this fight.

Delgado threw a lazy jab. Sonny slapped it away.

"Keep moving," shouted Brooks, "stick and move."

Sonny snapped out a jab, reddening Delgado's nose, but he danced away before Delgado could shoot one back. No percentage in tangling with him yet, not until he was tired.

Real man gets in there and bangs, said the monster.

Gets his butt kicked for no reason, said Sonny.

People think you're scared, said the monster, of a walking jar of steroids.

Someone shouted, "Sonny the Dancin' Bear." Laughter.

No one's hitting them. The bell was drowned in boos.

In the corner, Brooks said, "Pick up the pace, make him run after you."

Delgado's dark eyes bored into him, daring him to stand and slug it out, but the smile was gone, his mouth too busy sucking air.

Jab . . . seven and hop back. Jab . . . three and sidestep, keep moving, changing direction, make him move. All those miles running on the Res and in the park were paying off now. I can dance forever and Delgado's legs are losing their spring, his gladiator chest is heaving, all those fancy muscles are screaming for air, jab . . . five . . . five, he's winding down like a toy with a dying battery. The crowd was beginning to catch on now—they could see the plan, figure out the ending. Delgado knew it, too, and he couldn't do anything about it.

By the fourth round, Delgado was lurching after him on stiff legs, his entire body heaving for air, his dark eyes pleading with Sonny to stand still, make a target.

"Take him," yelled Brooks.

Delgado's head and neck were stone, from the waist up he barely moved under the hammering hooks, the right cross, the straight left, but his legs seemed to fold into themselves, like telescopes, and he went down like a man sinking into quicksand. His arms were ready to keep fighting, but he couldn't get up.

"Smart fight," said Brooks, as Martin hoisted Sonny's arm in victory. "You controlled it all the way."

They all drove back to the Witherspoons' apartment. Betty and Denise were waiting at a table loaded with cake and soda and a six-foot hero sandwich. They had expected him to win. Brooks stayed just long enough to make a toast.

"To the future heavyweight champion of the world."

Nobody laughed. In the sudden silence, they all turned to Sonny.

"If he wants it badly enough," said Spoon.

"Amen to that," said Johnson.

Sonny shivered. He felt a movement in his chest. Like wings rustling.

On his way out, Brooks pulled Sonny to one side. "Remember what you been doing right. It works outside the ring, too. Just be cool. Whatever happens."

"What does that mean?"

"You'll figure it out when you got to." Brooks pulled his pistol out of his jacket pocket and slipped it into the holster at the small of his back. "Gotta go to work. You call Jake?"

"Now?"

"Right now. He's waiting." Brooks was out the door.

Martin shambled over, his cheeks bulging with sandwich. "Thawasomefie."

Sonny had an urge to hug him, but he said, "Can I use your phone?"

Martin swallowed. "If she's got a girlfriend for me."

"I want to call Jake. Be okay with your folks?"

"Of course." Martin looked surprised. "Jake's got a telephone."

"Why not?"

"Well, um, I thought, he's a, you know . . ."

"He's got a VCR and a microwave. And a CB in his truck. You thought we used smoke signals?"

Martin stuffed the rest of the sandwich into his mouth.

Jake picked up on the first ring. "How'd you do?"

"Fourth-round kayo."

"What took so long?" Jake chuckled.

"Guy didn't want to get hit."

"Can't blame him. What'd Al say?"

"Said I fought a smart fight. Controlled it."

"Real good, Sonny." The old man's voice was relaxed and warm. "When you fight next?"

"Friday night."

"Save me a good seat."

When he got back to the party, they were all at the dining-room table listening to Johnson. He sat at the head of the table, tugging his beard and speaking in a deep, measured voice, as if he was addressing a class. "The amateur road is the road for Sonny—give him the gradual progress, the ring experience and the media exposure he needs as he matures physically and emotionally. Win the Gotham Gloves, then the citywide Golden Gloves, national Golden Gloves, come back from the Olympics a twenty-year-old man with a gold medal, ready to turn pro."

"What if he wants to turn pro now?" asked Martin.

"Forget it," snapped Johnson.

"It's his life," said Denise. She looked embarrassed when everyone turned to stare at her.

"It's economics, young lady," said Johnson. "Be too long and hard a road as a pro now. Have to fight in small clubs, tank towns for bad pay in worse conditions. Have to fight whoever you can get, wild kids who can hurt you, old bums make you look bad without teaching you anything. Ain't worth it. And who's going to pay your way? Some gangster?"

"What if he was bankrolled by people who really believed in him?" asked Spoon.

"Who'd gamble on a kid?" asked Johnson, rolling his eyes to the ceiling. "A fortune on somebody who could lose interest, fall in love, go junkie on you. The amateur road is the only way—develop slow but sure. Alfred wasn't blowing smoke, Sonny could be heavyweight champ if nothing gets in the way. Mr. Donatelli should of seen this boy. Whoa." He wiped his eyes.

Spoon's eyes were wet, too.

"Sonny Bear-Kwame Hicks."

"Yo." A big kid with cannonball shoulders flashed a gold-toothed smile. "Who's this Yogi Bear? From Jellystone Park?" The men around him cackled and slapped their legs.

"I seen this before," said Johnson. "Ignore him."

"How you ignore Kwame Hicks, the next Gotham Gloves champ?" asked Kwame Hicks.

"Retard champ," said Martin. "Soup for brains."

"Shut yo' mouth, blubber," said one of Kwame's handlers.

"Shut Kwame's mouth," said Martin. "All that yellow in there matches his spine."

Kwame cursed and started toward Martin. Sonny felt the heat rise up his legs into his gut. Old pal, the monster, the evil spirit, welcome. Sonny stepped in front of Martin and smiled at Kwame. "You want to do this here and now?"

Men were suddenly pushing Sonny and Kwame to opposite ends of the room, and Spoon was pushing Martin out the door. Johnson laughed as he kneaded Sonny's shoulders. "I seen this before. You got yourself a real assistant trainer there, reminds me of me and Alfred."

"Hey, Tonto, I'm on the warpath." Hicks did a clumsy imitation of an Indian in an old-time cowboy movie. The men around him whooped and slapped fives.

"Just look at me, Sonny," said Johnson. "Hands!" He taped Sonny's hands. "If Kwame got to try to upset you in here, he can't be too confident for out there. How you feel?"

"Okay."

"Hey, Injun, any squaws back home looking for a real man?"

Johnson turned to one of the older men around Kwame. "Can't you keep that silly boy quiet? Ain't you got no pride?"

"Pride? Why ain't you training a brother, 'stead of some half-breed honky Redskin?"

A new voice said, "Because this young gentleman's going to be heavyweight champion of the world."

Brooks looked tired, his eyes were ringed with black circles and his clothes were wrinkled, but his voice had a cutting edge.

"Maybe if you brothers"—he drew out the word sarcastically—"concentrated on training Kwame to be a boxer instead of a motor-mouth fool, he wouldn't have to try to win his fight in the locker room." Brooks dropped a hand on Sonny's shoulder. "How you feeling?"

"Good." It was true. Brooks made him feel stronger, surer. And the monster bubbling up was part of it. Control the monster, use the monster, the fire was his partner.

The door banged open and a bloody-nosed fighter swaggered in, surrounded by grinning men. "U-nan-ee-muss," one of them said.

The man with the clipboard barked, "Bear-Hicks on deck."

"Just decide what you want to do and do it," said Brooks. "Take control. Of yourself. Of the fight."

Take control. Of yourself. Of the fight. He felt the monster, wings beating in his chest.

Let's do it. Together.

At the bell, Sonny hurled himself across the ring before Kwame could get his hands up and nailed him with a hook to the chin. He pivoted to throw a right but never got the chance. Kwame fell over like a tree.

Johnson screaming, "Corner, corner," reminded him to get to a neutral corner while the ref counted to ten. Might as well have counted to twenty. Kwame managed to get to his knees, but was stuck there.

Martin was in the ring, hugging him. "Hook . . . one." And Johnson was saying, "This is a record, must be some kind of a record."

Sonny looked for Brooks.

"Had to get back to the stake-out," said Johnson.

Strobe lights popped during the fight with Traynor, a tall kid with wraparound arms. Every time Sonny moved inside to hammer his body, Traynor tied him up. His ropy arms were hard as cables, and they squeezed the energy out of Sonny's arms.

"On your horse," said Johnson. "Hit and run, don't let him tie you up."

He tried. But Traynor was an octopus, and there was no way he could get close enough to hit him without being trapped in his tentacles. Sonny felt his power ooze away. He was pushing his fists, not firing them. The velocity was gone.

"Don't give up," said Brooks between rounds. "You can win this one if you just keep going."

It was a slow, grinding fight, the crowd booing all the way. He won the decision because he landed more effective punches than Traynor did, but there was no pleasure in the victory.

"Stunk," he said on the way to the dressing room.

"Got you to the semis," said Martin.

"Experience," said Johnson. "A hundred different styles, you got to see them all. Next time you fight a octopus, you know what to do."

"That was control, too," said Brooks. "You just hung in there, didn't quit, didn't go crazy."

Jake was waiting in the dressing room with a thick envelope. "She sent a plane ticket. Wants you in Phoenix this weekend."

"Got a fight."

Jake shrugged, stuffed the envelope into his trunks and pushed him out to arms' length. "You lookin' good, Sonny. Startin' to look like a Brave."

19

BROOKS AND JOHNSON plowed a path for Sonny through the fans and reporters packed in the corridor leading to the dressing room. "Sonnee, puh-leese." A hand shoved an autograph book in his face. Brooks brushed it away. Martin and Jake struggled to stay close behind.

"Sonny Bear." A young man wearing a press badge around his neck tugged Sonny's sleeve. "How do you feel about Indian rights?"

Brooks pushed in between them. "Ask him about Indian lefts. He's here to fight, not talk politics."

"Who are you?" asked the reporter, but Brooks had already pulled Sonny away.

The guard at the dressing room barred Martin and Jake. "Only two handlers per fighter for the semifinals. Commission rules."

Martin shook his hand and said, "Jab . . . seven . . . five."

Jake raised the Running Brave fist.

In the dressing room, TV cameras poked glass snouts at Sonny undressing, and fuzzy gray microphones on six-foot poles wormed their way between him and Brooks.

"Get used to this, Sonny," said Brooks. "Gonna get worse."

"We hope." Johnson laughed and slapped Brooks' palms.

Johnson took his time taping Sonny's hands and kneading the muscles of his back and arms. Brooks stood in front of Sonny to block his view of the door. It swung open every few minutes with a blast of crowd noise to let a fighter in or out. They all bounded out into the arena, psyched for battle, but only half of them bounded back in, high on the adrenalin of victory. Some were helped back to the dressing room, weeping and bloody. One was carried in.

"Don't look," said Brooks. "Talk to him, Henry."

"Keep your mind on Velez, he's a banger, but you can take him." Johnson's voice was steady, low. "Big, not as strong as he looks, but he can absorb punishment."

"A catcher," said Brooks.

"He's willing to take three to hit you once,"

said Johnson. "He'll keep coming, boring in, trying to get you to stand and slug, toe to toe. Macho man. I seen this before."

"Don't fight his fight," said Brooks. "Fight your fight."

"Fight smart," said Johnson. "Stick and move. Wear him down. If he gets inside, you tie him up."

"Like the octopus did you," said Brooks.

He knew they were talking to keep him focused on the fight, but loose, and he felt strong and confident. If Brooks and Johnson thought he could take Velez, he could think so, too.

"Sometimes you can learn more from a lousy fighter like Traynor," Johnson was saying, "than a real good fighter."

"I must of been a helluva teacher," said Brooks.

"Your problem, Alfred, you had a lousy assistant trainer." They slapped palms again.

"Bear-Velez, on deck."

"How do you feel?" asked Brooks.

His mouth was dry and his stomach was queasy. "Ready." He jogged in place and shook his arms.

Johnson said, "Let's rumble."

The door banged open to a blast of crowd noise, boos laced with jeering whistles.

"They'll want blood," said Brooks. "Don't listen."

"Bear. Go."

They went down the aisle three abreast, Brooks and Johnson moving him along with their shoulders, through a tunnel of sound into the glare of the ring lights. Velez was waiting for him, tall and massive, grinning down. "Indian boy, where's your tomahawk?"

Sonny raised his left glove. "Here."

They glared at each other during the referee's instructions. Velez' eyes were small and deeply set in his flat face. His nose had been mashed to a twisted button, his eyebrows were white braids of scar tissue. He must have fought a lot for an amateur, thought Sonny. Got hit a lot, whispered the monster. Imagine him with numbered squares. A punching bag for us. We'll give him some punishment to absorb.

Velez marched out at the bell and presented his flat face as a target too tempting to resist.

Jab . . . five . . . seven rocked Valez back on his heels. This is going to be a short night, dish

173

face. Right . . . eight turned his head into the flight plan of hook . . . one, on the chin, a short sweet tomahawk that would have rattled his teeth and crossed his eyes and knocked him flat if it ever landed, but it was still in the air when a concrete block slammed into Sonny's face and a battering ram smashed into his gut.

Sonny fell backward against the ring ropes. They held him up. He would have fallen without the three velvet-covered cables that sagged against his weight, then burned across his calves and back and shoulders as Velez pumped sledgehammers at his chest and arms, looming over him, silhouetted in the blazing ring lights, a grotesque shadow thrown up on the gym ceiling, drawn on a page in the sketchbook, a strange nightmare beast pounding him against the ropes that held him in place for the dark shape to punish.

His feet began to slide forward as his body was forced almost horizontal on the ropes. Hot sweat sprayed off Velez and burned his chest.

"Sonny. Sonny."

He wondered if he was already unconscious, having hospital dreams of a smiling blond girl. He felt sad for himself. So helpless.

Let everybody down. Brooks and Johnson and the Witherspoons thought he'd be heavyweight champion and Jake thought he'd be a Running Brave.

He was nothing. He felt small and alone, a little boy in buckskin selling jewelry outside Sweet Bear's Kiva.

"Sonneeee." It sounded like Doll. He must be unconscious.

The referee was peering down at him, ready to stop the fight if Sonny looked helpless. He was shaking his head. Right thing. Am helpless.

"Sonneee." A piercing whistle, a needle of sound through the dizzying roar in his ears. Two pinkies in her mouth.

Doll's whistle.

"Fight back, Sonneee. You can do it."

It was Doll.

Somewhere out beyond the lights. Got to get up. See Doll.

Help me, monster.

Help you?

You owe me one, all the trouble you put me through.

You dumb Redskin, who do you think I am?

A Hawk, an evil spirit, a passive-aggressive personality? I am you.

I'm the monster, thought Sonny. It's me. Control it. Fear and fury. Make it work for me.

It started at his toes scraping for leverage on the canvas, a tingling strength that built speed as it rushed up his legs and into his stomach and chest, out his arms.

He threw his arms around Velez, clamping the pumping arms to Velez' sides. Like the octopus did to him.

Velez struggled in his arms, then stepped back. Sonny held tight. Velez took two more backward steps, lifting Sonny off the ropes, up onto his feet.

"Sonneee, way to go, Sonneee."

He was closer to Velez than he had ever been to her, chest to chest, jaw against jaw, in a fierce clinch, holding on until his eyes focused and the swirl in his brain slowed into thought.

"Wanna fight or kiss?" snarled Velez.

The referee thrust his arms between them and pried their bodies apart. Thousands of voices screamed for action. He tried to isolate hers. Could he have imagined it? The bell rang. He lurched to his corner.

"Smart," said Johnson, massaging his chest. "You got out of a real tight spot."

"Now you got to fight your fight," said Brooks, dribbling water into his mouth.

"Stick and move."

"Control, take control."

"He'll be cocky now," said Johnson. "Use that."

Velez came out grinning for the second round. He did a mocking little Latin dance step into the center of the ring and acknowledged his friends' cheers with a wave. At the bell Sonny lunged forward, fired a stiff jab at the twisted button nose and jumped away. Velez shook his head and waited for the next punch, but Sonny was already circling behind him. Velez whirled and Sonny popped him again. Velez stopped and set himself for a barrage, but Sonny had reversed direction.

"Go, Son-nee, go."

He had to force himself not to search for her. Chop wood. Concentrate. Take control. Fight your fight. Stick and move.

Concentrate. Tune out everything else. Kick the stick and hold the tea in your mouth and breathe through your nose.

One more time, a stinging jab that made Velez grunt, the first acknowledgment of pain. I'm getting to him. But don't wait to be trapped again. Move. Leave him flat-footed. Make him turn to find me. Jab . . . three, dance away. He's looking stupid. Jab . . . seven, sidestep. He can't stand this. Jab . . . five . . . five. The crowd laughed at Velez.

"Wake up, Chico."

He wanted to rush Velez, end the fight now with a whirlwind of combinations, pop-pop-right-pop-pop-BANG, that would drive him through the ropes, piercing whistle, where are you, Doll?

NO. Control. Stick and move, jab and dance away. Velez' nose was a bloody button and his lips were twisted with frustration and his eyes had disappeared into fleshy caves. He wasn't hurt, but he was angry because he was looking bad.

"Good job." Brooks and Johnson swarmed over Sonny in the corner. "This is it. He'll go nuts on you."

"Just stay cool. Wait for your time."

"Then give him the tomahawk."

Velez roared out for the third round on a

thunder roll of crowd noise, and he threw up a windmill of punches. Sonny backed and circled, knocking the punches away, letting his arms and shoulders absorb the blows he couldn't avoid. Velez was desperate to regain the crowd, to squash him. Sonny almost felt sorry for Velez, so out of control.

One minute into the round, Velez dropped his hands for an instant to rest and grab air, and Sonny nailed him with a right that jerked his head back. Jab . . . five turned his face back into another right that left him open for the hook.

Indian boy, where's your tomahawk?

Here.

Everyone in the arena saw it coming, including Velez. No one moved. Including Velez.

He was out before he hit the canvas.

Sonny looked for Doll as the referee raised his arms in victory, but Martin was hugging him and Brooks was saying, "You did it, Sonny," and then two new fighters were in the ring and Johnson was steering him back through a thicket of hands reaching out to him, "Attaboy, Sonny. . . . Way to go, champ . . ." and the guard at the door winked and let Jake and Martin into the dressing room packed with reporters and cameras. TV lights made the room as bright as the ring.

20

"WHERE YOU FROM, SONNY?"

"You really an Indian?"

Faces bobbed up in front of him, asked questions, disappeared.

"What tribe?"

"This your chief here?" A camera swung to Jake.

"Sonny Bear your real name?"

He couldn't understand why anyone would be so interested in where he was born or the size of the Reservation or that his full name was George Harrison Bayer and that he'd been named for his mother's favorite Beatle. They wrote down all his answers. Martin was giving an interview about the importance of their training on Rocky, and Jake was telling a camera that Moscondagas had fought in every American war since the French and Indian.

"Brooksy Baby!" A bull with flashing diamond teeth barreled into the room.

Brooks yelled, "Elston," and they hugged.

Reporters began interviewing each other. "That Elston Hubbard?"

"When was he champ?"

"Isn't he on a TV series now?"

"Yeah. Who's Brooksy Baby?"

The cameras turned on Hubbard and Brooks, the fuzzy gray mikes hovered above them. Reporters asked them questions. Sonny caught snatches of the story. Hubbard had beaten Brooks in Brooks' last fight, twenty years ago, a slugfest people still talked about because Brooks refused to go down even though he was way overmatched. Hubbard's son had just won his heavyweight semifinal. He'd be fighting Sonny for the Gotham Gloves title.

The reporters seemed to love the story. Hubbard was loving the attention.

"My boy versus Alfred's boy," boomed Hubbard, "the continuation of a quarter-century grudge match. Everybody write that down. Shoot it on tape. Two great kids for the title. That Sonny Bear is smart and tough. But is he smart and tough enough for Elston Hubbard Junior? Buy tickets and find out."

The photographers posed Brooks and Hubbard hands up, scowling, as if they were about to continue their old fight. Then Elston Junior was posed with Sonny. They were about the same size.

Then Junior posed with Brooks, and Sonny posed with Hubbard, who whispered, "Never pass up publicity. Remember that."

Brooks winked at Sonny. He looked proud and happy.

When the photographers finally left, Johnson untaped his hands. "This is really something, Sonny, really something. If only Mr. Donatelli could see this."

They left the locker room in a laughing, chattering clump, Jake and Martin and Brooks and Johnson around him. The corridor was still filled with fans.

"You were wonderful, Sonny."

She looked thinner, blonder. Her face was bright with crimson lipstick and baby-blue eye shadow. His stomach turned over and his mouth went dry. Her red dress clung damply to her body.

"I heard you out there," he said. His tongue felt thick.

"I know."

He felt as though everyone else had melted away. They were finally alone.

Words began forming in his mouth. Doll, let's go away. Together. Now.

"Great fight, Sonny," said Stick.

"What are you doing here?" Brooks' hand went to the small of his back.

Stick raised the snake head. "Come to see the fights. Law against that?"

"Stay away from Sonny," said Brooks.

"Does Sergeant Brooks tell you what to do?" asked Doll. "Or can you come out with us and celebrate?"

"He's got something else to do," said Brooks.

"That true, Sonny?" asked Doll. "Something else you want to do?"

He lost his breath. Everyone was staring at him. He was frozen. He felt Doll willing him to break away, to leave with her. He found his voice. "Some other time, Doll."

Brooks and Johnson grabbed his arms and rushed him out of the arena. He knew she would be in his dreams tonight, and that he dared not look back.

21

H E WOKE UP TIRED and cranky all that week, hung over with fleeting, jagged dreams. To chase the dark shadows he ran hard in the mornings, pounding through the park until his mind cleared, shouting birds and squirrels out of his path, whirling to throw windmills of punches at trembling bushes, scaring the park people out of their cardboard homes.

He battered Rocky in the afternoons, snarling at Martin to pick up the pace, to snap out the numbers louder, faster, in ever more complex combinations until his mind was purged of everything except pure action.

Movement in the gym would slow, then stop as he attacked the dummy. Other fighters would drift away from their mirrored images, leave the punching bags dangling, to gather around him, to grin and nod at each other. Hearing them murmur, Sonny's on edge, kid's ready to rumble, drove him to hit harder.

Johnson stroked his beard and looked pleased. The Punching Postman announced, "This boy has it, take it from me." Even the Fave seemed impressed. "Sonny Bear is the future."

He tried to exhaust himself during the day so he'd fall asleep early, not think about her. Sometimes when the phone rang at night, he'd shiver, thinking it might be her. But it never was.

Jake stayed at the gym for a few nights, then flew back to the Res to feed the dogs. Sonny missed Brooks. Johnson said he was very close to breaking his big case.

Martin invited him to move into his room for the last two nights before the title fight. He said they could watch old fights on the VCR.

The whole family watched with them, Denise peeking up from her homework, Betty from the papers she was marking. Martin's dad turned down the sound to do his own commentary. "Ali was the greatest, but you can learn more here from watching Joe Frazier. Ali did so many things only he could get away with, get you in bad habits. See how low he holds his hands, see how he backs away from a punch, instead of slipping it—you do that,

Sonny, it's lights out."

He didn't think he learned much he could use right away, but sitting in this warm place with people who cared about him made Johnson's amateur road seem truly possible, win the Gotham Gloves and the Golden Gloves and the Olympics, follow the path blazed by the champions on the screen. It was beginning to seem real.

The night before the fight, while Martin went to a friend's house to borrow a schoolbook, Sonny sat at his desk and doodled. After a while it became a drawing, a boxer running behind a hawk up a mountain road. He got lost in the picture.

"Hey! You're really good." Denise was standing beside him with tea and cookies.

"No, I, uh, just . . ."

"Don't crumple it up. Please." She put down the tray and picked up the drawing. "Where'd you learn to draw like this?"

"My mother's an artist."

"On the Reservation?" asked Denise.

"No, she lives in Arizona now." He was surprised at how easy it was to talk with her. She was pretty and nice and smart. He should feel the warms for her. But she wasn't Doll.

"You miss her?"

"Huh?" Did she know about Doll?

"Do you miss your mother?"

"Oh. Sometimes. I do. Maybe after this fight I'll visit her. She sent me a ticket."

"Maybe she'll come to the fight."

"No way. She hates me fighting."

"Then how come she . . ."

"Hey!" Martin stamped into the room. "Leave him alone. He needs his . . . You do this, Sonny? I didn't know . . ."

"You just don't know everything," said Denise. "His mother's a southwestern artist."

"The Hawk," said Martin, snatching the drawing out of Denise's hand. "The one Jake talks about. Follow the Hawk."

"What's that mean?" asked Denise.

"You just don't know everything," said Martin.

"Moscondaga fairy tales," said Sonny. "The Hawk is the spirit inside you."

"More to it than that," said Martin. "You got to let it out before it eats up your insides, destroys you. If you follow it, the Hawk leads you to your special destiny. In Sonny's case to

188

be a Running Brave, a sort of . . ."

"Jake's brainwashed you," said Sonny.

"You bet. He invited me to come up to the Res with you sometime. I'm going to tape his memoirs. For a book."

"Sonny can do illustrations," said Denise.

"Would you?"

"Let's win the fight first."

Martin stayed home from school the day of the fight to make Sonny a giant breakfast of bacon and eggs and muffins. They were sitting at the kitchen table, pleasantly stuffed, drowsy in the morning sun slanting through the window, when Martin asked, "Who was that girl?"

"What girl?"

"Come on."

"Some girl I knew."

"Was that guy her pimp?"

Sonny tried to keep his face expressionless. It was something he didn't want to think about. "Who said that?"

"Alfred told my dad she was bad news."

Sonny shrugged. "Don't know."

"You mean you don't want to talk about it."

"Right."

"She's really built."

"You don't quit, do you?"

"I'm a writer, not a fighter." He grinned.

"You better remember that." Sonny made a fist.

"You hit me it's a felony, your hands are weapons."

"Not till I turn pro." He stood up. "Might as well get you while I can."

"You wouldn't hit a guy with glasses, would you?"

"Never." Sonny snatched Martin's glasses and laid them on the table. "Now."

He was kneeling on Martin's lap, tickling him under the arms, when the phone rang. Martin was still cackling and gasping as he answered it. He swallowed suddenly.

When he hung up the phone, his face was twisted. "Alfred's been shot."

"Is it bad? What happened? Who . . ."

"I don't know. My dad just said to get there fast."

Spoon met them in the hospital lobby. "It's very bad. He took a load of buckshot in the back. If he hadn't been wearing his gun, he would have died instantly. As it is, he's paralyzed and they're worried about infection."

The elevator and the corridor were filled with police officers. Mrs. Brooks came out of a room and headed straight for Sonny. "He wants to see you."

Brooks' eyes were closed. Tubes ran out of his nose, his throat, his arms. Machines hummed and beeped around him. A nurse stood near his head. "A minute, that's all," she said.

Brooks' eyes fluttered open. His lips formed words, but Sonny couldn't hear them. He put his ear close to Brooks' mouth. He thought he heard the word "win," but he could have imagined it, could have thought that's what Brooks would say.

The nurse tugged at his arm. Brooks' eyes were closed.

"He's going to be all right?"

She looked away.

He walked out of the room on rubbery legs. He remembered how he had felt when the fat farm boy hit him in the groin. Gasping for air, for strength, trying to focus. He was glad when Spoon put his arm around his shoulders. "Did he say anything?"

"Told me to win."

"That's Alfred," said Mrs. Brooks. She started to cry. The police officers closed around her.

22

THE GUARD OUTSIDE the dressing room barred them all this time. "Not on the sheet." He pointed to a list of names on a piece of paper taped to the door. "Commission rules."

"This is Sonny Bear," said Martin. "He's fighting for the title."

"I know Sonny," said the guard, "but nobody goes in without your name on the sheet. I don't make the rules."

"Got to be a mistake," said Johnson impatiently. "Get the commissioner."

"Can't leave my . . ."

"You taking responsibility for this?" Johnson looked fierce. "If my boy loses because of you . . ."

The guard said, "Okay, Mr. Johnson, I'll be right back." He scurried off.

"I seen this before, Sonny," said Johnson. "They're trying to mess up your mind before the fight."

"They're scared of the tomahawk," said Martin. He held up his palms. "Stay loose, champ. Jab . . . seven . . . five . . . two. Never opened with that combination before."

The monster stirred, snickered. No mistake, Injun. They're not scared of the tomahawk. Journey's over. No Stonebird, no championship. Sonny felt suddenly sad. He wouldn't be able to win a fight for Brooks.

The guard returned with a man in a red blazer. "You're out, Henry. Didn't you get my telegram?"

"What telegram?"

"Bear's disqualified."

"Says who?" Johnson's fists came up. His body swelled.

"We got documents. Kid's had six pro fights. Upstate."

Johnson whirled on Sonny. "True or false?"

"Smokers," said Sonny.

"You take money?"

"Yeah."

Johnson's hands dropped. His body deflated. "Sorry."

"Late for that." The commissioner rapped his clipboard. "Some title fight you left me with. Have to put Velez in against Hubbard." He glared at Sonny and marched away.

"What're smokers?" asked Martin.

"Lousy little fights for has-beens and wanna-bes," said Johnson. "Should of told me."

"Didn't think of it," said Sonny.

"What's the big deal?" asked Martin.

"Rules," said Johnson. "If you take money, you're not an amateur no more." He leaned against the stone wall of the corridor. "Somebody out to get us. This never comes up 'less somebody makes a big complaint to the commission."

"Hubbard," said Martin. "Afraid of Sonny."

"No, even if they knew, they'd want to win in the ring. Somebody's out to wreck Sonny's career. And they did it, yessiree, they did it."

"No," said Martin. "It's not over yet."

"Is for me," said Johnson.

"We'll fight pro," said Martin. "We'll do it the hard way, be better, coming up through the tank towns, leaving a trail of broken bodies, right, Sonny?"

He had no more words. There was only one thing left to do.

"Where you going?" yelled Martin. "Wait for me."

23

THE TOW TRUCK came alive on the first kick.

"Where we going?" Martin was scrambling into the passenger seat.

"Get out."

"I'm your trainer, I . . ."

"No more boxing."

"I'm your writer."

"Do this alone."

"I'm your friend, Sonny." The owl face was serious. "I'm going with you. Where to?"

Sonny jerked the truck into traffic. "The Deuce."

"Them," said Martin. "The girl and the pimp. You're not going to . . ."

"Directions. Get us there."

He drove carefully. This was no time to be stopped by the police. Martin wasn't sure of the way, but he knew they had to head west to get back to Manhattan. Sonny kept the skyline in sight as he wove through deserted blocks of shuttered factories and side streets with rows of attached houses.

"You think he shot Alfred? You think he turned you in to the commission?"

The sky was dark. The lights of the tall buildings were stars to follow.

"Sonny. What are you going to do to him?"

"Watch for cops."

That shut him up. The river sparkled beneath them as the truck clattered over the bridge into Manhattan. Martin pointed downtown. Neon splashed the windshield. He turned onto Forty-second Street. Times Square. Bursts of music. They were in a valley of flashing lights. The stink of sick flesh.

"Reach into the dashboard."

"All those wires . . ."

"Won't hurt you. Deep as you can go."

"What am I supposed to . . . Hey." Martin pulled out the old Colt .45. "Is it loaded?"

"Better be." He double-parked the truck outside Chub's Grotto. "Stay here."

"You kidding?"

Sonny shut off the ignition and handed Martin the key. "Make sure Jake gets his truck back." He took the gun out of Martin's hand.

"Whatever happens."

"What does that mean?"

Sonny jammed the gun under his belt at the small of his back and covered it with his shirt. He climbed out of the truck and walked into Chub's.

"Sonny Bear!" Chub dropped a pizza. "Heard you been . . . Hey, you can't go . . ."

Martin was right behind him, around the counter and into the tiny bathroom, through the little door beside the toilet and into the chattering, clanging, screaming electronic battlefield of the video arcade, past rows of hunched bodies to the door marked POSITIVELY NO ADMITTANCE.

"Can't you read?" Mo loomed up.

"Stick said it was an emergency," said Sonny.

"Didn't tell me."

"Doll supposed to tell you."

Mo looked confused. "She didn't."

"Stick'll make her pay for that."

"Don't say nothing. Please."

Sonny pretended to think it over. "This time."

Mo unlocked the door.

In the darkness he sensed direction. He shut out the moans and whispers and slaps of flesh on flesh from behind the curtains, the mingled odors of sweat and ammonia, and concentrated on his destination. A Running Brave could smell Doll's sweet perfume, hear the tap of Stick's walking club.

He followed a trail that was inside his head, making turns that seemed the only way to go, down stairs, up stairs, around a corner, to a heavy steel door. It was open. Stick was waiting for him, the shotgun barrel pointing at his chest.

"Close enough." There was a pile of suitcases behind him. They were packing for a trip. Doll was sitting in a corner of the enormous brown velvet couch, wearing the red silk robe Stick had worn the last time Sonny was here. She cradled a baby in her arms.

"Hi, Sonny. Say hello to Jessie."

He felt heat in his neck and groin. Close that down. Push it away.

"What do you want, Sonny?" asked Stick. The snake's head was steady.

"Come to kill you," said Sonny. Martin gasped.

"It was him or me," said Stick.

"That's your business," said Sonny. "You narc'ed me."

Stick's brow furrowed. "What?"

"Don't try to weasel out of it."

Stick glanced over his shoulder at Doll. "What's he talking about?"

"You turned him in, Stick?" She looked puzzled. "For what?"

He turned back to Sonny. "What you trying to pull?"

"You called the commission." It works—Jake was right. People get confused, can think of only one thing at a time. "You told them about the smokers."

"Smokers?"

"My fights back home."

Stick was shaking his head. The snake's head wavered. "Didn't you fight tonight?"

"He was disqualified," said Martin. "For being a pro."

"Who's the fat boy?"

"My trainer. He's out of luck, too. 'Cause of you."

"Oh, poor Sonny," said Doll, rocking her baby in her arms. "Why'd you do it, Stick?"

"Wait a minute," said Stick. He glanced back and forth from Doll to Sonny. "You know this ain't my style. Stick is evil, but he ain't a snitch."

The snake's-head shotgun was still leveled at Sonny's chest, but the muscles of Stick's shoulders and arms were no longer so tense and ready. Watch for twitches, Jake had said, shifts in the eye, quick breaths.

Sonny said, "Can't believe anything you say. You pulled my chain from jump."

"Right thing," said Stick. "That's my game. I spotted you off the bus, a Native American, never trust cops, never rat on me."

Sonny willed his body to relax, his face to wrinkle into thought. "You didn't call the Gotham Gloves?"

"We were rooting for you—we'd've had a friend who was champ," said Stick. "Hey, man, if we weren't on our way out of town, we'd have come to the fight."

Sonny let his head drop. He shrugged. "Maybe you can help me get some money. Get out of town, too."

Stick relaxed. He smiled at Doll. "No hard feelings, Sonny. I'll give you the other half of that hundred. Even though you didn't make the delivery."

Sonny watched the snake's head dip toward the floor, but he waited until Stick exhaled with relief and let his shoulders go slack before he made his move, one long step forward on his left foot, a quick kick with his right. Stick yelped.

Sonny snatched the stick out of the air with his left hand and slapped Stick across the face with his right. Stick fell backward into the suitcases, scattering them. Sonny tossed the shotgun stick to Martin, who fumbled it but held on.

Sonny drew the Colt and put the tip of the barrel to the tip of Stick's nose. "Now, I'm going to kill you."

"No," screamed Doll. She hugged her baby. "No."

Sonny felt the wings rustling inside his chest. Yes.

Stick waved his spidery hands. "I got crazy money, man, I can set you up on The Deuce . . ."

"I'm gonna blow your face off." The monster filled him: Do it!

"Please don't, Sonny." Doll was crying.

"Don't do it, Sonny." Martin's voice was

high and tight. "Screw up your life."

Who is ordering you around now? asked the monster. Blow this piece of garbage away.

"You can't be a chief with blood on your hands," said Martin.

The wings beat against Sonny's ribs, pressed against his lungs. "Kill him for Brooks."

"That's not what Alfred wants," said Martin. "He wants you to be champ."

"That's over."

"We can do it, Sonny, the hard way, tank towns, tough fights." Martin's glasses slipped down his sweaty nose. "We'll turn pro for real."

Fat owl never shuts up, said the monster. "Shut up," said Sonny.

"Right thing." Stick sat up against the suitcases. "Brooks just wanted you to be his decoy." He wiped his bloody nose with silk underpants. Doll's? Push that away. Concentrate.

"Alfred and Jake want you to be a Running Brave."

"Ignore that fat fool," said Stick. "Brooks just wants you to be a rat for him."

"You gonna listen to a dope dealer set you up to get busted?" said Martin.

Stick and Martin began yelling and Doll

began to sob. The monster thrashed in his chest. Get it over with. Pull the trigger—don't you ever learn, half-breed? They rob the fights, they switch the rules, they kill off the people who care about you, Brooks, Dad, squeeze the trigger nice and easy, like Jake taught you. . . .

He thought of Jake and closed his ears and slowed his heart, the little death. Got to think now—what should I do, what would a Running Brave do, a warrior who can speak with wisdom, a peace bringer who can fight to the finish?

A Running Brave would know what to do. He would have remembered everything he learned on his journey, of mules and mushrooms, the selling of death to kids, a friend named James who survived a war to die on the streets at home. A Running Brave would remember and think and make the right decision for the People.

The noise in his chest drowned the screams in the room. How come they can't hear the monster? Jake's evil spirit. Brooks called it a passive-aggressive personality. Donatelli called it a fire. Everybody has a name for it.

The Hawk inside me.

"Stop," roared Sonny to the thrashing wings. "Leave me alone."

Their faces froze, they thought he was shouting at them. Why can't they hear the beating wings crushing my lungs, trying to break free. He gasped for breath. If I was a dumb Redskin, he thought, I could really believe there was a Hawk in there and this was the time to let it loose.

And follow it out of here.

He looked at them—Stick quivering, a cornered weasel; Martin clutching the shotgun stick, his shirt black with sweat; Doll heaving under the robe, her makeup bleeding down her cheeks. The baby, incredibly, smiled up at Sonny.

They were all waiting for him.

To take control.

He took a deep breath. Scalding pain. "Let's go. We're taking Stick out of here."

"Way to go," whooped Martin.

His chest swelled, the pain was unbearable, another moment and he would explode and die. His body shuddered from toe to scalp. He felt a sudden chill. And then calm.

The Hawk was free.

"Never make it," said Stick. "Guys out there won't let Doll out of here."

"Not taking Doll. Just you."

Stick smiled. "Doll won't let you do it."

"Sure she will." Sonny looked at her hugging her baby, her bird eyes pecking around the room for a way out. "She loves her baby. She'll do what she thinks is right for her baby." He thought about his mom. She must have called the boxing commission after reading about him in the newspaper. She must have thought that was right.

"Don't let 'em do it, Doll." Stick's voice was a low growl. "I'll get you."

She buried her face in Jessie's tummy. The baby giggled.

"Sonny." Stick's voice was hoarse. "She took your wallet and your pack. When the pigs jumped us in the Port."

Doll looked up. "I was keeping it for you, Sonny. I swear." She flashed the neon smile. "It's here somewhere."

"Keep it. Don't need it."

"You're such a good artist, Sonny. Maybe you'll draw Jessie someday."

"Maybe."

In the calm, his head felt very clear, his senses sharp. He smelled ammonia and pizza and exhaust fumes, markers on the pathway out. He heard the slap of flesh and the chatter of video games and the thump of trucks rolling over manhole covers on The Deuce.

Sonny pulled Stick to his feet. "Martin, once we're out that door, we keep going till we hit the street. No matter what happens."

"Got it," snarled Martin. It was almost funny, Martin acting tough. But he felt proud of him. Every Running Brave has a young warrior-in-training by his side.

"Give me the stick. Keep the Colt under your shirt till you need it. We're out of here."

He pushed Stick ahead of him. He turned at the door. Doll was rubbing her nose against Jessie's and cooing at her. He wondered if he would ever see them again. Sonny slammed the iron door.

They scrambled down the stairs, then up the other flight. In the corridor of curtained cubicles he linked arms with Stick and motioned Martin to do the same. They moved Stick along with their shoulders.

Mo loomed up. "What's going . . ." He

jerked back at the snake's-head stick. "Where's Doll?"

"Don't let 'em take me," squealed Stick.

"Doll's waiting for you upstairs," said Sonny. He never stopped moving. He knew Mo would step out of their way.

No one looked up as they rushed through the video arcade, into the little toilet and out into the Grotto.

Chub blocked the way.

"Don't let 'em take me," shouted Stick. "I'll drop the dime on you. They'll close you down."

Sonny jammed the snake's head into Stick's spine. "Anything goes wrong, you're gone."

"Let him go," said Chub.

Martin snarled, "Keep your head down and mouth shut if you know what's good for you, fatso." He tore his shirt pulling out the Colt, but once Chub saw it, the snakes and eagles on his arms seemed to shrink. He let them pass.

And then they were out on The Deuce.

"This your truck, boys?" A woman in a brown uniform was about to write a parking ticket. She looked them over sternly. Sonny poked Stick to keep him quiet.

"Sorry, officer," said Martin. "We had to

make a pickup. We'll move it right away."

"Let you go this time," she said. "You boys are real lucky."

They didn't let themselves laugh until Sonny pulled the truck out into the traffic on Forty-second Street, Stick jammed between them, clutching his bony shoulders with his spidery hands, moaning, the gun in Martin's hand deep in his ribs, and they couldn't stop laughing until they got to the hospital.

24

THE HILLCREST LODGE hall was smaller than Sonny remembered, a cramped box of a room, the whitewashed cinderblock walls covered with cheap plaques and moth-eaten animal heads. It looked more like a rec room than a boxing arena. For has-beens and wanna-bes. Most of the men were crowded around four kegs in the corner, filling their paper cups.

"I seen this before," said Johnson. "Fightin' in a outhouse."

"From the Outhouse to the Penthouse," said Martin. "The Sonny Bear story."

"Don't you ever zip up?" grumbled Johnson.

Sonny undressed in a storeroom jammed with folded card tables and softball equipment. Johnson double-wrapped his hands with thick gauze and heavy-duty tape. "Not gonna let you bust a knuckle in this hole. Stick and run the early rounds, don't head-hunt."

"Just what I told him last time," said Jake.

"If he listened," said Martin, "he wouldn't be on his way to the title now."

"Quiet now," said Johnson. "Let Sonny concentrate." He held up his palms. "Jab and hook."

Sonny snapped out the jabs and threw slow hooks, feeling the warmth spread through his body. Push everything else away and concentrate on the farm boy, and the crowd that came to see him grind the half-breed into red meat.

Don't think about Brooks, lying in that hospital three weeks now, just staring at the ceiling because he'll never walk again.

Don't think about Doll and Jessie.

Don't think about Mom, on her way with Roger's lawyer to make you come back to Phoenix with her.

Don't think about Stick, waiting for a trial at which you'll have to testify.

Just think about this fight.

The rematch, the second chance, the new start.

When the door opened, he pushed ahead of Jake and Martin and Johnson. He swaggered down the aisle, banging his big red gloves together, whipping his ponytail from side to side against his bare shoulders.

I'm back, bozos, and I'm stronger.

". . . main event, a grudge match we've all been waiting for. Winner take all, three hundred dollars, in black trunks . . . showing some real guts, let me say . . ." there was scattered applause. ". . . weighing one hundred and eighty-five pounds, the pride of the Moscondaga Nation, Sonny Bear, The Tomahawk Kid."

He looked around. Johnson was rolling his eyes and jerking his thumb at Martin, who was grinning and slapping palms with Jake.

"And from Hillcrest, the undefeated champion of Van Buren County . . . The Fighting Farm Boy . . . Glen Hoffer. . . ."

Hoffer lumbered into the center of the ring and waved to the cheering crowd. The curly yellow hair on his chest was already glistening with sweat.

"Looks like the fighting furbag to me," said Martin.

"Don't ever make light of a fighter," said Johnson, "especially if you're not one."

Sonny listened carefully to the referee's instructions. I'm a pro now. It's for real. Not a kid from the Res making a few bucks. Not an amateur. First step out on the road to the top.

The crowd started calling for action right away, but Sonny ignored them. Jab and move. Control the fight. Make Hoffer tired and frustrated. The crowd booed at the bell.

"Smart round," said Johnson, as Martin trickled water on his tongue and Jake rubbed his back. "Now pick up the pace. You're a pro now, an entertainer."

Martin shouted, "Jab . . . five . . . five," as Hoffer marched after him on flat feet. Late in the second round Sonny landed a sharp combination that rocked him, but he lingered too long admiring his punches. Hoffer clinched, grabbing him in a powerful bear hug that gave the farm boy a chance to drive a knee into his groin and rake his laces across his back. Sonny felt the sting of torn skin. As the referee separated them, Hoffer rammed his head into Sonny's mouth, splitting his lower lip. Blood dribbled down his chin.

Don't get mad, get even. Jab and move. Work the farm boy, don't show him you're hurt.

Sonny slipped two jabs in a row, but Hoffer grabbed him again and kicked his shin. Control. Take what you got to take till your time comes.

It came in the third. Hoffer threw a round-house right that Sonny ducked. He dropped into a squat as the big punch whirled over his head. The force of the punch pulled Hoffer into a half-turn, his right glove flung over his left shoulder, his big face exposed.

Jab . . . five . . . seven . . . two. Right . . . eight. Hook . . . one.

Bingo.

Sonny strolled to a neutral corner. He was almost sorry it was over. At least one more round. Too soon, it was over too soon. He wanted to savor it a little longer, remember every punch. It was going to get harder now, it was for real from here on in, tank towns and short money on a hard road, crazy kids and losers who wanted to hurt him, a long climb. But he was going to make it.

"Winnah . . . by a knockout in two twenty-one of the third round . . . Sonny Bear . . . The Tomahawk Kid. . . ."

The crowd cheered politely. They were disappointed, but respectful.

Martin hugged him. "Un-dee-fee-ted."

Johnson pulled him out of the ring. "I seen this before. Let's split. Jake'll collect."

Sonny pulled his pants over his trunks while Martin draped his jeans jacket over his bare shoulders. They hurried out ahead of the crowd to the parking lot. Sonny started the truck and gunned the engine until Jake climbed into the cab with the money. It was a tight squeeze, the four of them. Sonny burned rubber out of the parking lot. Martin started whooping first, and then they were all yelling and laughing.

"Tomahawk Kid. Where'd you get that?" asked Sonny.

"I'm a Writing Brave," said Martin.

Sonny looked at Jake. The old man made a fist, the thumb thrust up between the knuckles of his third and fourth fingers.

Halfway down the mountain, at the fork, Sonny asked, "Which way?"

Jake said, "Don't matter. Both take us there."

"Straight to the title," said Martin.

"Never seen this before," said Johnson.

Turn the page for a sneak preview of the
next novel in Robert Lipsyte's groundbreaking
The Contender boxing saga,

WARRIOR ANGEL

A thought began to tug at the corner of Sonny's mind, but before he could decide whether or not to let it in, the door banged open and a voice boomed, "The world is waiting for Sonny Bear. Is Sonny Bear ready to deee-light the world with another deee-fense?"

Malik and Boyd jumped up and the trainer and the cornermen straightened. Even Red Eagle turned.

"Mind if I keep shooting, Mr. Hubbard?" asked the cameraman.

"My life is an open screen, dedicated to the cham-peen." Elston Hubbard gently slapped Sonny's cheeks. "Awake, my man, and prepare to pummel another pretender to the throne." He snapped his fingers at the trainer. "You know better. He should be warmed up by now."

"He won't do nothing, Mr. Hubbard," the trainer said.

Sonny watched as the big round dark face loomed over him. He smelled Scotch and cigars. For once it didn't sicken him. Nothing. I am beyond feeling.

"Ten thousand people outside that door, Sonny, the cream of Las Vegas and Hollywood, and countless millions at home, waiting to be inspired anew by the Tomahawk Kid, the Natural Man, the Native Son. Can't disappoint." He grabbed Sonny's shoulders and pulled him off the table. He held up his hand. "Jab."

Sonny threw out a left. It felt as though he were punching through water.

"I said jab."

The second one was straighter but barely moved Hubbard's open hand. "Navy Crockett gonna think you are trying to pick his nose. JAB!"

He aimed this one at Hubbard's face and tried to remind his muscles to snap it out, to fire from the shoulder, to roll his wrist on impact.

Hubbard inclined his head, and the jab shot over his shoulder. "Better."

The cornermen took over, rubbing his arms, setting up targets. Sonny began jogging in place. He felt his muscles warming up, but they seemed detached from his brain. Someone else's muscles.

The door banged open. "Let's go. Crockett's in the ring."

"Showtime," said Hubbard. "Lead the way, Red Iggle."

It wasn't until they were out of the dressing room that Sonny realized they had been inside the health club of a casino hotel and were now crossing the pool area toward the parking lot. The air was warm, moist. He needed to breathe through his mouth as well as his nose.

Red Eagle, in the lead, scattered ashes from his steel bowl along a red carpet that ran through the crowd to the ring. They passed between two rows of young women in bikinis waving rubber tomahawks and shouting, "Son-nee, Son-nee."

Hubbard waved to the crowd, urged them to pick up the chant. Hands reached out to touch Sonny. He saw faces of people he knew, movie actors, rappers, ballplayers. Why were they here?

Navy Crockett was waiting in the ring, taller than Sonny and thirty pounds heavier, some of it fat. His upper arms jiggled when he shook them over his head. He spotted Sonny coming up the ring steps and glared.

As he climbed through the ropes, Sonny thought, What's his problem?

Sonny's robe was stripped off. The trainer ran an ice cube down his spine. He felt Hubbard's strong hands on his arm. "Snap out of it, Sonny. This . . . is for . . . your title."

Hubbard smacked him across the face, hard.

Sonny tried to will himself out of the brown murkiness that surrounded him, banging his gloves together, whipping his head from side to side so his ponytail slapped his bare shoulders. But the lines to his feelings had been disconnected.

The voice of the ring announcer could have come from another planet as he introduced the celebrities. They paraded across the ring, touched Crockett's gloves, touched Sonny's, wished both men luck. The former champion, Floyd (The Wall) Hall, raised his hands to the crowd. Lights glinted off a gold ring on every finger. The rapper glided across the ring to hug him. When the movie star trotted across the ring, the crowd shouted his alien-killer line from the movie: "Sayonara, snotface."

"And now, the main event, for the heavyweight championship of the world . . ."

The trainer's fingers were deep in the muscles of his shoulders, and the cornermen were kneading his legs.

"In the green trunks, the challenger, from Ja-mai-ca, at two hundred forty-one pounds, the Reggae King, Nay-veeeeee Crock-ett."

Steel drums pounded in the darkness at the back of the parking lot and a line of dancers snaked around the ring.

"In the red trunks, the pride of the Moscondaga Nation and of all Americans from Native to new, the youngest heavyweight champion in history, at two hundred ten pounds, the Tomahawk Kid, Son-neeeeeeeeeeee Bear."

War drums thundered, and the Tomahawk Girls shimmied down the aisle. Steel drums, war drums, the shouting dancers, the stars and the ballplayers and the rappers standing and cheering.

Sonny thought, I can't breathe.

ONNY LOOKED AWFUL, DRUGGED, A ROBOT. He lurched out to the center of the ring, hands down, chin out. If Crockett hadn't been stiff with fear, he could have marched up and nailed him, ended the fight right then.

Look at those idiot managers, jumping up and down, yelling at Sonny to lift his hands, go after Crockett, chop that lard ass down. Do they want him to lose, or are they as stupid as the boxing writers say? They aren't much older than Sonny, punks who worked for that slimeball Hubbard. Why did Sonny let them in? Because he's losing his grip. Because he doesn't know who his real friends are. Because he needs me.

The crowd screamed for action.

PJ slipped onto the couch next to Starkey. "That was so cool, the way you got out of Circle. Which is the one you're rooting for?"

"Red trunks," said Starkey.

Roger plopped down. "Crockett's scared. Why doesn't Bear just put him away?"

Because I want all this to end, thought Starkey, thinking for Sonny, because I want to be free, to go back to sleep, to be alone.

A voice on the TV cut through the murk.

"Navy, stick, stick and move, Navy."

"That guy used to train Sonny," said Starkey, "back when Alfred, Henry, and Jake were still in his corner." They didn't need to know all this. But he couldn't stop talking about Sonny. "That was all before Hubbard's punks took over."

"You know so much about him," said PJ.

"Starkey is obsessed with Sonny Bear," said Roger.

"We're not allowed to diagnose in the Family Place," said PJ.

"It's an observation, not a diagnosis," said Roger. "There are people who fixate on stars because of a lack in their own—"

"Shut up!" The words came out like straight rights and shut Roger right up.

A jab bounced off Sonny's forehead, just enough to shake him, not enough to hurt. Starkey felt pressure over his left eye.

Sonny looked blank, unfocused. Starkey imagined that Sonny's mind was wandering, seeing faces from his past floating in the crowd, attaching themselves to bodies, then moving on, like masks on strings. Mom and Doll and Robin, Alfred and Marty and Jake.

He imagined that Sonny felt dreamy now, surprised that his body could move on its own, as if it were acting out highlights from old fights. Remember how we kept moving to the left on Boatwright so he couldn't pull the trigger on his jab, in and out on Velez, who was dangerous but dumb.

One of the TV commentators said, "Crockett's got too much reach. Sonny has to move inside if he wants to win this."

"He's having trouble just keeping his hands up," said the other one.

"Sonny, look out," screamed the idiots in the corner.

Suddenly, Sonny was on the ring floor and the referee was pushing Crockett into a neutral corner. Starkey tried to feel Sonny's shock and pain, but felt only numbness. Was that all Sonny was feeling too?

The steel drums smothered the sound of the referee's count, but Starkey could see him mouthing the numbers. "Two . . . three . . . four . . ."

"Up, Sonny, get up," screamed Starkey.

"Stay down, Sonny," said Roger. "You get up, it's just more of the same."

He wanted to slug Roger, as big as he was. He started to rise, felt PJ's body stiffen. He held the tension for a beat and thought, If Roger is a member of the Legion of Evil, if he is the adversary sent up from Hell to test me on this Mission, does it make sense to engage him now? Do you beat the devil early or late?

The bell rang.

"Sonny is saved by the bell," snorted Roger.

You, too, thought Starkey. I will not engage you now. This is about Sonny right now, not about me.

Hands dragged Sonny to his stool, snapped an ampule under his nose, poured ice water on his head, dropped a cube down the front of his trunks, massaged his arms and legs.

The camera moved in. Starkey saw the boom mike, a fuzzy fat gray caterpillar hovering over Sonny's head, picking up the conversation in his corner.

"Wake up, Sonny." The trainer was slapping his face.

"What's your name?" A man in a suit and tie. The ring doctor.

"Sonny Bear."

"Where are you?"

"Las Vegas."

"Who you fighting?"

"Navy Crockett."

The doctor shrugged and walked away.

One of the idiot managers said, "Sonny, you got to back off—"

But the other idiot said, "In his face, get right up in Crockett's face—"

And then the trainer said, "Tie him up."

Too many voices in Sonny's ear, Starkey thought, when all he needs is mine. He said, "Just hang on."

"For dear life." Roger laughed.

The bell rang.

Bolder now, Crockett marched right up and fired a jab. Some distant memory must have jogged Sonny to slip the punch, let it fly harmlessly over his shoulder, to ram a short right uppercut into Crockett's soft belly.

"Huuunh." Crockett doubled over, his chin slamming into Sonny's shoulder. Sonny grabbed him, pulled him into a clinch. Crockett wrenched loose and stumbled away.

The fear was back. Crockett circled again. The movie stars and rappers and ballplayers stamped their cowboy boots and chanted,

"Son-nee, Son-nee."

Behind them, to the steel-drum beat, voices from the cheaper seats chanted, "Nay-vee, Nay-vee."

Starkey could sense that Sonny's murkiness never completely cleared and that he never quite connected with his body, even when he got his hands up and began to move his feet. Twice he caught Crockett coming in with sharp jabs. The second time he managed to land a hook as Crockett was backing away. It startled Crockett, and he tripped over his feet, falling on his backside. He was up again before the referee could start the count, but he stayed away from Sonny for the rest of the round.

The crowd began to boo through the middle rounds as the fight fell into a pattern. Crockett would circle until he gathered enough courage to attack. He might land a jab or two, even a brief flurry of punches, but Sonny would trap his arms and step into a clinch.

The referee broke them apart as quickly as he could, "No hugging—fight," but Crockett couldn't stop Sonny from clinching.

One of the TV commentators said, "Navy's too slow, too set in his ways to figure this out."

"He's a classic plodder willing to absorb punches to give some back," said the other. "But Sonny's hardly mounting any offense at all. Wasn't this supposed to be a just a little tune-up fight for the champ?"

At the beginning of the tenth, Starkey sensed Sonny's murk beginning to lift, like a stage curtain slowly rising. He could see that Sonny felt it first in his arms, lighter, then in his feet, moving faster. Sonny snapped three straight jabs into Crockett's face, driving him back across the ring, and as the crowd began to roar, he slammed a left hook into Crockett's jaw and a vicious short right into his heart. Crockett fell against the ropes, his elbows snagged on the top strand. The crowd was on its feet as Sonny lowered his head and pounded Crockett's soft gut.

"Kill the body and the head will die," shouted Starkey.

Roger snickered. "Where you hear that dopey stuff?"

Starkey started to rise, but PJ squeezed his arm and he settled back down. It was in The Book. Mr. Donatelli had spoken those words to Alfred, who had passed them on to Sonny.

Can't react to Roger, not now.

Crockett had nothing left, he was in no condition to box for twelve rounds, and he sucked air and circled until the final bell sounded. The crowd was booing and whistling. It got louder after the ring announcer pulled down the mike and read the judges' cards.

Split decision. Sonny wins, retaining the title.

Starkey felt sweet warm relief fill his chest.

"Crockett got robbed," said Roger. "And your guy is almost as screwed up as you are."

"Get lost," snapped Starkey.

Roger stood up. "Make me, psycho pup."

Defining moment, now or never. Starkey stood up. He tried to imagine what Sonny would do, but before he could even think it through, the heel of his hand shot out and slammed into Roger's nose. Roger sat down hard, blood leaking between his fingers.

Roger whimpered. "I'm gonna tell—"

"And I'll say you bothered me," said PJ. "Now get lost, toad."

PJ didn't wait for Roger to leave before she sat down and hugged Starkey. He was too surprised to resist. Besides, he knew Roger would

15

snitch to Dr. Raphael that he had hit him and they'd send a counselor up.

Then I can get back to my room and send Sonny another message. He closed his eyes and wrote it in his mind: *Dear George Harrison Bayer, Saw you on TV after the fight. That look in your eyes, like it's hopeless. It's not. Hang on. I'll be there as soon as I can. Warrior Angel.*